NORTH NOTTINGHAMSHIRE

SHORT STORY COMPETITION 2017

Sherwood and The Dukeries

First published 2017 by Bookworm of Retford
1 Spa Lane, Retford Notts. DN22 6EA
www.bookwormretford.co.uk

ISBN 9781999833404

Designed by Burgess Design and Print
Printed by Imprint Digital

These short stories are works of fiction
and are not representations of historical fact.

A catalogue record of this book is available from the British Library.

CONTENTS

WINNERS

from left to right:
Lesley Middleton 2nd prize,
Pamela Mann 3rd prize,
Elizabeth Carney-Marsh 1st prize

FORWARD

SANDEEP MAHAL

Director for Nottingham
UNESCO City of Literature

Nottingham was awarded the UNESCO designation as a City of Literature on account of the city's literary heritage, its international outlook, its diverse writing community, and its commitment to improving literacy across the city. It is therefore a great pleasure to be writing this introduction for the exceptionally talented writers of this year's North Nottinghamshire Short Story Anthology.

Winning the UNESCO title took a lot of hard work: work demonstrating that Nottingham and Nottinghamshire is full of diverse voices and talent. This anthology shines a spotlight on those new voices and talent. It celebrates the most imaginative and amazing short stories from writers all across North Nottinghamshire. Within this collection of short stories, we find pressing proof of literature's capacity to bring us new ways of looking at things. These are stories that you will want to tell other people about, ones you can't stop thinking about, stories you will want to read again.

I hope this anthology encourages more people to write their own stories. For more tips and inspiration, I would recommend The Short Review website which has recommended collections and links to sample stories.

One of the other best places to start, in terms of events, is to check the Nottingham City of Literature website – we have a listings page with regular updates of all the literary events, talks and workshops happening in Nottingham.

And, of course, you must write and keep writing. Ultimately, writing is a solitary art. But you can learn a lot about your craft, and benefit from the stimulus and camaraderie of other writers, by joining writing groups such as Nottingham Writers' Studio, which supports writers at all stages of their careers. They host workshops, events, networking and social gatherings, and they are able to provide advice and support on things like publishing, literary agents and the like.

Our status as a UNESCO City of Literature is a permanent one. This is a great honour, but it also places an obligation on our city to nurture and support the development of literature. Our mission is to 'Build a Better World with Words'. We plan to use the UNESCO accreditation to boost our profile on the international stage

as a city with a rich literary past, a vibrant contemporary scene and a very exciting future – a future where Nottingham becomes a leading cultural destination for the enjoyment and study of literature.

I am delighted that audiences locally and internationally will be able to enjoy some of the biggest and most exciting short story writers of the moment. We strongly support this unique and spirited publication and wish you continued success.

Sandeep Mahal

Director of UNESCO
Nottingham City of Literature

ELIZABETH CARNEY-MARSH

BONNETS TO BREECHES

1ST PRIZE

Writing *Bonnets to Breeches* has been a truly fulfilling experience. It is my first attempt at writing and was born from a desire to tell the stories that have otherwise been lost throughout the years.

Having retired from teaching music due to my health, it has been a real joy exploring another creative outlet such as writing, and I must say I have fallen in love!

The idea for *Bonnets to Breeches* came from my time volunteering in The Walled Kitchen Garden at Clumber Park and starting to hear the wonderful stories almost lost to time. Through conversations and research about not only the estate but the Women's Land Army, I was able to form a historically accurate backdrop in which to place my fictional story.

I owe a great debt to the team of staff and volunteers, whose knowledge and love of Clumber ignited a spark in me, and the belief of my partner, family and friends for their unwavering support and endless proof-reads.

The stories of the Women's Land Army are in real danger of being lost forever. These women were trail-blazers and explorers of their time. This story is dedicated to them, The Women's Land Army, formed one hundred years ago, in 1917. "God speed the plough and the woman that drives it."

BONNETS TO BREECHES

CHAPTER 1

LEAVING LONDON

I remember the glass, cold on my forehead as I leaned on the window, looking out at the dark city disappearing before me. I had never been out of London before. I knew I was going north to the county of Nottinghamshire; the rest was a little vague. I wondered, with a hollow, clawing feeling in my chest, what my parents were doing right now. It was late and my father would have closed the Pharmacy for the day and sorted deliveries and scripts for the following morning. Mother would have got tea ready and they would be eating by a single candle so as not to invite the Zeppelins.

Would they shout my name up the stairs like they sometimes did, calling me down for supper? Or would they be cross that I hadn't helped either of them do the jobs that needed doing? When would they find my letter? Oh God, what had I done? I didn't want to cause them any more pain than they had already been through, losing my brothers Sydney and Harry in the hell of war. But I could no longer be the good little daughter keeping house whilst my brothers risked everything for something they believed in. Something I believed in.

I saw the recruitment poster asking for girls to join the newly formed 'Women's Land Army' whilst out with Mother. There it was, as clear as day, in the window of the Post Office. 'National Service' it said, 'Women's Land Army'. In the centre, a woman in uniform pushing a horse-drawn plough. Doing her bit for King and Country! 'God speed the plough and the woman who drives it' it said. This was what I wanted to do. Mother saw what I was looking at. "Don't even think about it, Clara Moon. For a start, you wouldn't know one end of a horse from the other!" I protested, as I often did, but to no avail. Mother and Father had already lost two children to the war and poor Teddy was still fighting on the front. I was hardly let out of their sight and according to Father, "Girls need to be at home".

The following day, I offered to do errands for Mother on my own as I knew she was busy with Father in the pharmacy. She agreed – partly because I timed my question at a time when she was particularly flustered! I took the dismissive "Very well, just get on with it" as permission granted and set off. I took the bicycle and did Mother's errands in double time. This left me plenty of time to call at the Post Office on my way home. The postmaster, Mr Beaty, was a grumpy old soul, but kept himself to himself. His wife, however, wanted to know everyone's business and delighted in passing the information around the neighbourhood. So I loitered around the front of the store until Mrs Beaty was sent on an errand in the back. I hurried up to the counter and asked Mr Beaty in a hushed voice for the enrolment forms needed for the Women's Land Army.

"Now, Miss Clara Moon, I never had you down as a country girl," said Mr Beaty to my surprise. The man had never said more than a few words to me in all my time visiting.

"I...I...well...it's..." I stumbled clumsily over my tongue.

"No need, Miss Clara, I find it quite a thing. Quite a thing. I suspect your parents are proud?"

"Well..." I stared to panic.

"No fear, Miss Clara. It is the business of a postmaster to keep his customers' privacy." I sighed with relief. "The business of a postmaster's wife, however..." His raised eyebrows were signal enough for me to collect the forms he quickly handed me and exit as swiftly as possible. For the first time ever, I heard Mr Beaty chuckle as I hurried out of the shop and the admonishment from Mrs Beaty for her husband's sudden jovial nature and a demand to know what had happened in her absence. I remember smiling as I heard him say, "Postmaster business, my dear, postmaster business," and her disappearing into the back of the shop with a huff.

I filled the forms out in secret at night in my room. Every day thereafter, I intercepted the postman to look for news. I think Father was getting suspicious of my unusual new pastime. I told him I was waiting for letters from Teddy. The awful truth was, we hadn't heard from Teddy in some months. The letter finally came with my appointment time, for which I was required to attend the WLA recruitment office in the centre of London. The weeks that followed passed in a whirlwind of half-truths and hidden preparations. I'm still not quite sure how I managed to go through the whole process without my parents finding out, particularly as we were such a close family.

The day finally arrived when I was expected at the railway station at 8pm. I had spent the day with my parents, doing jobs, running errands and trying to etch the images of their faces in my mind to take with me. I had to do this; I needed to do this. I told them I was off to Marjorie's house to pay a visit on my closest friend, who lived on the next street. In reality, I sneaked my pre packed bag from under my bed and headed quietly out of the front door.

The clawing feeling in my chest would not leave me as the train hurried North that night, further and further from my home than I had ever imagined I'd go. The cold of the glass numbed my forehead as I stared out at the darkness. Silently I prayed that I had made the right decision.

CHAPTER 2

ARRIVING AT CLUMBER -- MARCH 1917

The station at Worksop appeared early the following morning, with shafts of dawning sunlight piercing the clouds of steam like bullet holes in tunics. As I stepped onto the platform, this small but perfectly formed station seemed to welcome me like no other.

"Well, it certainly isn't King's Cross, is it?" a voice from behind said.

I turned and saw a beautifully styled woman lighting a cigarette beside me. "No, a tad smaller, I'd guess," I answered.

The woman laughed and stuck out her hand for me to shake.

"Cecilia Ellington. You can call me Sissy," she said confidently with a big draw on her cigarette.

"Clara Moon," I said, shaking her free hand whilst juggling my case.

"Business or pleasure?" Sissy said with a wry smile.

"Hopefully a little of both," I answered. "I'm being billeted at Clumber Park with the Women's Land Army." That was the first time I'd said it aloud to someone and it was both frightening and exhilarating at the same time.

"Well that, Miss Clara Moon, is fantastic news! Me too!" Sissy said this with a beaming smile I shall never forget. It was infectious and we stood there grinning at each other until we were interrupted by a short, elderly man with a flat cap low over his face.

"You'll be the women then?" he said gruffly, and I sensed he wasn't too happy to see us.

"Last time we looked," Sissy answered with raised eyebrows and a twinkle in her eye, which elicited a small smile from the grumpy gent.

"Well, I'm here to take you to Clumber," he grunted.

"Fabulous!" said Sissy. "I only have a couple of bags, if you'd be so kind?"

"I should think if you're going to be handling the backside of cattle, there's nowt'll bother ya about those two bags." With that he walked off, leaving Sissy speechless, which, even though I'd only known her a few minutes, I had the feeling was a rarity.

***

We bounced around in the back of the truck, desperately clinging on to both ourselves and our luggage all the way there. It was a slow, bumpy journey but one that delivered the most breath-taking of views. I still remember that feeling of wonder, looking back at the entrance to Clumber through the back curtains of the truck, and then being engulfed by the most magnificent row of lime trees that seemed to stretch forever. Through heathland and forest, we continued for some time until our truck stuttered to a halt. Walter, our driver and guide extraordinaire, beckoned us to join him outside. We had obviously reached our destination.

As I jumped down, I was taken aback by the magnificent house that stood before me. Large, elegant archways housed doorways and windows, and in places there were beautiful statues in arched enclaves. Above these lay impressive sash windows, which must have held superb views onto the gardens and lake beyond. The church sat behind the house and its bell tower stood tall in the blue morning sky. Lawns were perfectly manicured and Sissy and I could only stare in wonder at its beauty.

"That isn't where you're stayin', Missus; that's the Duke and Duchess's residence. You'll be in the stable yard. Follow me." Walter trudged off and we followed, still numbly taking in our surroundings. We were led into the stable yard and shown to a corner building. There we were met by Mrs Thornley, who turned out to be Walter's wife. The Duke and Duchess had kindly paid for Mrs Thornley to be our housekeeper and her daughter Alice our maid, during our time at Clumber.

Mrs Thornley showed us up a wooden staircase to two rooms joined by a single door. In the first room were two bunk beds and in the second, three, enough to sleep the ten girls who had been billeted here at one of the first WLA training schools of its kind. The room was bustling with activity and it looked like we were the last to arrive.

"Right then, girls, you will find your uniforms on the end of your bunks. Lunch will be served in an hour, which should give you plenty of time to get settled and dressed in your uniforms. Mr Thornley will be taking you up to Home Farm, where you will meet Mr Davey, who will set out your training schedule. Any questions, ask later. Alice will sort out anything you need or may be missing bedding-wise. See you downstairs in the kitchen in an hour." With that, Mrs Thornley abruptly left. The silent room bustled into life.

Introductions were excitedly and hurriedly made. As well as Sissy and I, there were Betty, Agnes and Flo from the west of the country, Dotty and Nancy from Manchester way, and Evelyn, Margaret and Norah from the other side of London to me. Sissy and I would share the last remaining bunk by the window. I took the top bunk as Sissy had a habit of walking in her sleep apparently! The uniform was folded neatly on the end of my bunk.

There was a moment of trepidation slipping on those breeches for the first time, along with the smart shirt, tie and jumper. As I donned the stockings and tied my shoes I could not stop the grin from spreading on my face. This was it: this was what I had waited for. I pulled on the overcoat and lastly came the hat. I held it in my hands, staring in wonder at the badge on its front. I belonged. For the first time in my life I felt I was doing something worthwhile. I remember thinking I would never wear a skirt or petticoat again if I could help it. There we were, ten smart, intelligent and brave young women ready to take on the world, all staring at each other with enormous grins on our faces. The joy I felt at that moment I would never forget as we noisily ran down the stairs to our new world beyond.

CHAPTER 3

FROM PHARMACY TO FARM

The previous day we had been introduced to Mr Davey, who had shown us with much pride around Home Farm. The stench was quite something, but he assured us our nostrils would adjust. I don't think Sissy was convinced. The farm was home to eighty-nine Highland and short-horned cattle, one hundred and eighty-three sheep, thirty-eight pigs, nine horses and numerous poultry. There were also acres of arable land growing a range of root crops. Our first task that morning was learning the art of milking cattle, or so we thought. We were up at five o'clock and Mrs Thornley assured us our breakfasts would be waiting for us after our first lesson of the day. I can honestly say that the excitement and elation of the first day had dimmed somewhat in the early morning darkness.

As Walter dropped us off at the farm Mr Davey came to greet us.

"Right, first job is mucking out. Grab a fork and follow me." Mr Davey clearly wasn't a morning person.

The following three hours we spent mucking out stables and pens. A few of the girls were sick with the stench, but were soon told to pull themselves together. I discovered that it was better to breathe through your nose, as taking a gulp of air through your mouth was akin to eating a mouthful of what you were shovelling. The animals were mostly cooperative, although I did regret not putting my boots on as my shins would be black and blue by this evening. At 8 o'clock we were collected for breakfast. All of us were silent as we shovelled the warm oats into our mouths, desperate to rid them of other tastes. Once finished, I and several of the girls hurriedly changed into our boots for our next session on the farm.

We returned to the farm, to be put into pairs. Sissy and I, as now seemed the custom, teamed up together. We were given a milking stool and a bucket and led to 'our cow'. Mr Davey didn't give the girls names but Sissy and I discovered, over the years, cows are far more cooperative if you can have a good chinwag with them whilst milking! So we named ours Poppy, after our Poplar roots in London. Sissy insisted on going first, having said she'd seen it done before (although I have my suspicions this wasn't quite true) and that it "looked a piece of cake"! As she perched herself on the stool and placed the bucket under Poppy's udders, she gave her hands a fierce rubbing-together. I looked at her quizzically.

"Us girls never like cold hands, I'll have you know, Clara Moon!" With this she rolled up her sleeves and gave a firm pull with both hands. At that precise moment Poppy let out a disgruntled noise and shifted her whole rear end out, which knocked Sissy flying off her stool and into a pile of freshly mucked-out dung. I don't think I had ever laughed so much in my life up until that point. I rushed over to see if Sissy was OK with tears running down my face. Her shocked expression soon turned into laughter, too, as we and the rest of the girls had to be bought back into line by an unhappy Mr Davey.

It's fair to say there's quite a knack to milking and it took some time to perfect. Some girls were naturals; others not so much. There were plenty of other skills and jobs to master, though, including harvesting, threshing, haymaking and ploughing, amongst caring for the other animals on the farm. Ploughing the fields with the horses was backbreaking work at times, but the fresh county air and midday sun filled you with joy. It was sometimes hard to remember why we were doing what we were. The country was running out of food: the men that once worked this farm were away at war. In that first three months of learning all those skills, I had the time of my life. Part of me felt incredibly guilty for the elation in my heart, knowing that Teddy was out there somewhere and Harry and Syd would never again feel the sun upon their faces.

At night, I often lay on my bunk, exhausted from the day's labour but insistent on writing home several times a week. I wondered how Mother and Father were doing, how life in London was, what with the constant threat of bombs and Zeppelin attacks. I wondered what their reaction was when they realised I had gone. I wondered if the reason they hadn't replied to my many letters was because they hadn't arrived, or they were just busy. I wondered if they ever read my letters at all. Deep down, though, I knew I had disappointed them, when all I ever really wanted was to make them proud like my brothers had done. Even though the replies never came, I never stopped looking out for news whenever Walter returned from town. And every time he saw me, he would shake his head and say, "Not today, Miss Clara."

CHAPTER 4

THE WALLED KITCHEN GARDEN

After a few months of working the farm and the field, Sissy and I were called in to see Mr Davey. He explained that the gardening staff in the house's kitchen garden were depleted due to men at war and we had been chosen to go and support and learn the skills to grow produce that would feed not only the family and guests but the estate and surrounding villages, including Hardwick, where Home Farm was located. We were told to report to the Head Gardener, Mr Barker, at 5am the following morning.

Before the sun had a chance to rise, Sissy and I were up, dressed and walking from the stable yard up to the kitchen garden. The Walled Kitchen Garden at Clumber was close enough to walk from our billet and our bones were grateful for no more truck rides from Walter. We made our way to the bothy behind the walls of the great glasshouse we had been told so much about. There, waiting for us with his pocket watch in his hand, was the formidable Samuel Barker. Mr Barker had been Head Gardener at Clumber since 1899 and commanded great respect from all over the estate and beyond. The Duke of Newcastle had built him a house especially, to entice him into the job because of his mastery of growing chrysanthemums. The Duchess demanded a fresh flower daily on her dressing table all the days of the year.

"On time. That's good," he said as he flipped his watch shut and placed it back in the pocket of his waistcoat. “Well, I’m not going to pretend this is an ideal situation, but the need arises. You will primarily be weeding and harvesting. You will be schooled in pruning, particularly the fruits along the walls as well as in the glasshouse. You will be under the instruction of Mr Dawes. He will give out your jobs for the day as well as teach you what you need to know. Mr Davey assured me you were the fastest learners in your women’s group. Let’s hope he’s right, eh?” With that he turned and walked off.

We stared after him for several moments, a little in awe and a little in fear, to be truthful. Without a word to each other we knew that this would be a man we should try not to displease.

“Which one’s which?” We spun and turned to the deep male voice behind us.

“Sorry?” Sissy said.

“Which one of you is which? Names?”

“Oh, erm, I’m Miss Clara Moon, sir, and this is Miss Cecelia Ellington.”

“Sissy, sir,” she said boldly.

“What did you call me?” he thundered loudly.

“No, no, sir. I meant people call me...” Her stammers were cut off by his roars of laughter.

“I know, Miss Cecelia, just having some fun,” he chuckled as he thrust out his hand and shook hers, then mine. “A pleasure to meet you both. I’m Robert Dawes and may I say what a great thing you are doing. My brother’s daughter has joined the WLA and I couldn’t be prouder. Now, let’s show you around. In fact, we may just be in time.” He started to walk towards the back of the glasshouse.

"In time for what, sir?" I asked.

"The magic, Miss Moon," he said with a wink. We followed him to the rear of what he told us was the palm house. He reeled off facts and details lovingly, like he was bragging about his favourite child. It was still early dawn as he unlocked the rear door. The first thing that greeted me was the most amazing smell. Fruits, flowers, bulbs and blossom filled my nostrils in an overwhelming wave. It stopped us in our tracks.

"You all right, ladies?" he asked with slight concern.

"Yes, Mr Dawes. The smell is just quite something," I said.

"Aye, a little different to cow muck, I expect," he said with another wink.

As he led us through the palm house and into the large open space of the conservatory my eyes didn't know where to roam first. Glass corridors disappeared for what seemed like miles either side. He opened the doors onto the garden and, as if choreographed by some higher power, the sun began to rise over the garden walls beyond. Sissy and I could only stare in pure wonder as the early morning sun seemed, as if by magic, to bring this incredible place to life.

"It's beautiful," I whispered.

"It is," he said simply.

In that one single moment, I was changed forever. I felt a peace I had never felt before, a reverence and an excitement. I knew right then that somehow within these walls I had come home.

***

As the weeks passed, my skills and love of vegetable gardening grew along with the produce I was cultivating. I quickly moved from weeding and harvesting to tending to the soft fruits, for which

Mr Dawes said I had a keen eye and flair. The glasshouse was hot and the work sweaty as the weeks pushed into June. I had a morning routine now of watching the sunrise over the far walls and then watching the colours of the garden change at sunset as it fell behind me – all from my front row seat on the steps of the glasshouse. Mr Dawes would often catch me sitting alone, contemplating how much life had changed. He'd shoo me back to the billet, always with a friendly nod and a "Goodnight now, Miss Clara." It was a ritual I had grown to love just as much as the garden itself.

It was on such a night that I sat on the steps, thinking about the latest unanswered letter I had sent to my parents. I had also written to Teddy several times and had got a reply, about which I was so elated. I'd re-read his words and wondered how much was bravado. I knew he was on the front lines and I could tell that things were not as they should be. I thought by joining the Land Army I would be doing the same as my brothers and contributing to the war effort. In one way I was, but oh, how different our circumstances! He saw the mud of the trenches stained with the blood of his friends. The only mud I saw was from the beautiful gardens before me: the splashes of red from the stalks of the rhubarb and the leaves of the kale. I'd give anything for Teddy to be brushing Clumber soil from his trousers than that of Flanders fields.

My thoughts that evening were broken by the sound of running footsteps coming from the Ducal Walk. I stared along the long range borders to the bottom gates and was shocked to see Sissy running as fast as she could. What was she doing? We were certainly not meant to use the Ducal Walk for cutting short the journey from the billet to the garden, and she knew it.

"What the devil...?" said Mr Dawes, who had walked up behind me. Breathlessly Sissy came to a stop before us.

"Clara, it's Poplar..." She gulped the air like water.

"Sissy, slow down, what's happened?" I said with a sense of confusion.

"I've had a telegram from Ma and Pa. Clara, Poplar has been hit."

"Zeppelins?" I whispered.

"No. Planes, planes with bombs, Clara. Broad daylight. Upper North Street School. All the children. And the buildings around. All over the East End." My head started to buzz with fear. "The Pharmacy was hit, Clara. Your mother and father...I'm so sorry."

CHAPTER 5

LOSING POPLAR

The train journey was a blur as countryside turned into city. My dear friend Marjorie met me at the station and tried in vain to explain what had happened. Poplar had indeed been hit. It appeared the Zeppelins had been replaced by planes, and the night-time attacks by day-time atrocities. Several bombers dropped their payload all over the East End of London, with Poplar worst hit. The school was destroyed whilst full of children. And Sissy was right: my home, too, had gone.

Marjorie and I stood before what had been the Pharmacy and my place of birth. The shop was completely destroyed, with rubble and medicine bottles strewn along the street. There was a gaping hole that opened up into the kitchen at the back of the house. The dining table miraculously still stood. I slowly clambered over bricks and charred wood to reach the back room. I stared wordlessly at the table where for years our family had sat and eaten together. Laughed together. Talked together. I sat down at the table once more, alone with only devastation for company.

Mother had died instantly. Father had held on and was taken to hospital. My train was too late to say goodbye. I went anyway, in the desperate hope the news was wrong and I could tell him how sorry I was and how much I loved them both. In the end, I held his cold hands and said those words to ears that could no longer hear and a heart that could no longer feel. For some time I sat, his cool hand clasped in mine held softly against my cheek.

Sitting at that dining room table, I replayed the feel of his hand on my face and the words I had spoken. There was a tin on the table which I never remembered being there before and I blew the charred ash from its surface and opened the lid. Inside were my letters. Lovingly bound with Mother's ribbon. They looked as though they had been read again and again as the paper was crumpled as only hands could. Underneath the bundle of letters was the enrolment photograph I had sent them in my uniform. I turned it over and in my mother's handwriting it said, 'Our Clara, a member of The Women's Land Army, March 1917'.

I closed the lid softly and kept the tin and its precious cargo safe as I collected as many other keepsakes from the rubble as I could. That night, I stayed with Marjorie and her family, who had welcomed me with open arms. They had even offered me a permanent home should I wish to stay. My thoughts turned to Teddy and the need to be here waiting for him to return home. But what home? I had a decision to make and one my soul was too tired to bear that evening. I loved my life at Clumber, but I wanted to be here for Teddy when he returned. The choice made demons dance in my dreams as I tossed and turned that night.

CHAPTER 6
HOME

In the end, the decision was an easy one. I boarded the train at King's Cross the day after my parent's funeral and said, what I knew would be a final goodbye to Marjorie and her family. I was going home. I had decided that Poplar would forever haunt me and if Teddy returned, I would like to think he would come to Clumber and enjoy the haven that I, too, had found there. I had written a long letter to Teddy explaining what had happened to Mother and Father. I told him of my intention to make Nottinghamshire my home and that I would very much like him to join me there on his return. I described the wonder of the Walled Kitchen Garden, how I could envisage him working the land with Mr Dawes and milking cattle with Mr Davey and how the fresh Nottinghamshire air would soothe his cordite- ridden lungs. I just prayed the letter found him safe.

The train journey seemed so much longer than that first time. I was desperate to see everyone again – a group of people who I had begun to love like family. I craved the safety of those garden walls, the familiar feel of the soil on my skin, the scent of the blooms filling my lungs and the taste of fresh fruit devoured straight from the tree. As the train pulled into Worksop station, I could see Walter waiting for me, cap in hand.

"Good gracious, Miss Clara, it is very good to see you," and just as I had stepped from the carriage he embraced me in a tight hug. Tears welled in my eyes as I dropped my case and hugged this kind old man in return. He held both my shoulders and looked me up and down as if inspecting the back of his truck for damage.

"I'm fine, Walter," I said.

He replied with a trademark grunt, "Very well," and with that he scooped up my bag before I could object and walked to his truck. I dutifully followed as he placed my case in the back and I got ready to climb in.

"No, no, Miss Clara, you can ride up front with me." And before I had time to answer, he disappeared around the side of the truck and clambered in. I joined him in the passenger side and we exchanged smiles as he started her up.

It turned out that the front of the truck was just as uncomfortable to ride in as the back. To me, it was the ride of my life. I could not wait to see the girls or the garden again. The last two weeks had felt like a lifetime. As we approached Clumber it dawned on me I had never entered the estate facing forwards – always staring out from the back of a truck! I sat straighter in my seat and looked out for that beautiful entrance. I think Walter could sense this, as he slowed as we approached. The beautiful cream stone shone in the afternoon sun and, as we passed through and down the hill, the magnificent row of lime trees greeted me with stunning wonder. Like a parade of soldiers welcoming me home, they stood tall and proud celebrating this magnificent place.

As Walter pulled into the stable yard I could see a gaggle of Land Girls with sun-bleached hair, flushed faces and filthy from head to toe. They turned at the sound of the truck and exploded with squeals and laughter, running towards me. The door was yanked open from the outside and I was pulled from the cabin by several hands.

"Clara!"

"You're home!"

"Give her some room, ladies!" I heard Sissy cry as she pounced on me and gave me a muddy hug. I couldn't help but laugh at their response.

"How are you, Clara?" said Evelyn kindly.

"I'm OK, thanks, Evie, just a little tired. So glad to be back and see your filthy faces!" Laughter and giggles exploded once more with me being taken by the arm and into the billet. Walter had carried my bag upstairs and as I unpacked, the girls got washed and changed. Today was Saturday, which meant all had the afternoon off. I was apparently being taken on a welcome home picnic.

That afternoon was as heavenly as the previous weeks had been hellish. The sky was a perfect baby blue and a cool breeze drifted up from the lake. We sat in the fields and shared our deepest hopes and silliest dreams. Sissy was the centre of attention as always, but this time not from her own making. She was being teased mercilessly by the other girls. It appeared, in my absence, Mr Davey's son had returned from convalescing at the hospital in Welbeck after a battle injury bought him home. It transpired that whilst I was away James Davey and Sissy had become smitten with each other. I had never seen Sissy so totally undone. I couldn't help but smile as I sat back on the warm grass and watched these incredible young women who, I knew, would be lifelong friends.

As we wandered back to our billet close to sunset, I told the girls I'd catch them up. There was one place I was still aching to see. I closed the wooden gate quietly behind me and I turned slowly. I drank in the orchards, the rows upon rows of crops, the fruit trees hugging the beautiful burnt-orange walls. I filled my lungs with the smells of the garden. I made my way along the front of the glasshouse, staring hungrily through the windows, hoping to catch a glimpse of how things had moved on whilst I'd been gone. I reached the steps on the entrance and sat. Hugging my knees tightly to my chest and watching the colours change as the sun fell behind me, I knew I had made the right decision.

I'm not quite sure how long I sat there. All I remember is that familiar footfall approach behind me and the lovely deep voice of Mr Dawes.

"Goodnight now, Miss Clara," he said softly.

I rose and turned to smile. "It certainly is, Mr Dawes, it certainly is."

CHAPTER 7

MISSING

I hadn't quite realised how much I had missed my life at Clumber and I threw myself back into the daily routine. As summer faded into autumn, the crops changed with the weather and it was time to harvest the apples, so the girls came up from the farm to help. The garden was filled with laughter and chatter, but only when the coast was clear of Mr Barker and his pocket watch. We stacked apples in racks as high as our heads in the fruit store day after day until the trees and orchard floors lay bare.

The girls returned to their farming duties, whilst Sissy and I remained in the walled kitchen garden. That was our first winter at Clumber and it was harsher than any of us would have imagined. We would wake in the darkness and return to our billet in the darkness. The short trousers of summer were replaced once more by our breeches, stockings and overcoats for extra warmth. The girls on the farm continued milking, no matter what the weather, and in fact enjoyed the warmth generated by the herd. They would huddle extra close and take their time over milking on those cold winter mornings.

For Sissy and me in the garden, we were never short of jobs. The glasshouse made work all year round and our winter jobs included cleaning vines and potting young plants ready for the next growing season, including cucumbers and tomatoes. We planted early potatoes and sowed early melons and the Duchess still wanted bouquets of flowers and bunches of grapes. The garden kept the house and estate in constant supply.

As winter slowly melted into spring, the garden sprang to life once again. We spent our days tying melons, propagating, top-dressing and a whole host of new skills we added to our list. Snowy days occurred even into April, but this did not stop us from potting-off spring-struck geraniums, top-dressing the cucumbers and sowing turnip seeds. We had been at Clumber for over a year now and we had all learnt so much. Even though the horrors of war had irreparably wounded my heart by taking my family, it was slowly soothed by the changing seasons spent inside the walled garden. I would regularly include this fact in my letters to Teddy, hoping beyond hope that he would join me here when he was able.

Thankfully, the summer passed without incident or disaster, unlike the one before. We continued to work the farm and the fields with as much enthusiasm as we started with. We were also truly part of the estate family now, and were respected in our own right for the dedication and competency we bought to any task given to us. Sissy and James were very much an item and James had asked for Sissy's hand in marriage. She instantly said yes, but insisted they wait until the war was over and her work with the Land Army complete.

It was a late September evening and I'd had my orders from Mr Dawes to head back to the billet. I didn't take much convincing, as it had been a long day in the glasshouse and I was ready for my bunk. The girls were back from the farm and Sissy was already in bed writing home to her parents. I was greeted by tales of the day and bursts of laughter. I quickly washed and changed into my nightclothes just as a knock came at the bedroom door. We all stopped and looked at each other quizzically – no one ever knocked this late. Evie opened the door and Walter stood the other side.

"Sorry to bother you, ladies. Miss Clara, there's an urgent telegram for you." I jumped down from my bunk, went to the door and reluctantly took the telegram from his hand. The girls surrounded me with worried looks on their faces. I stared down at the telegram in my hands, 'The War Office' emblazoned on the front. My stomach turned for what news maybe held inside and I stumbled backwards as my head spun. I remember the arms of friends guiding me to a lower bunk. I remember the feel of the paper on my weather-worn hands as I opened it. The words blurred into one with by brain only processing parts. 'Private Edward Arthur Moon...Missing presumed dead...Belgium...so sorry...'

I don't remember how long I cried, but I remember the arms of the girls holding me close whilst sobs racked my body. I don't remember falling asleep but I must have, as I woke in my bunk with tears dried on my face and the crumpled letter held tightly to my chest. I stared at the ceiling of our dorm and wondered how, when surrounded by so many people I loved, I could feel so desperately alone. I did the only thing I knew that would help me through losing my dearest Teddy: I donned my uniform, walked to the garden and placed my hands in the soil.

CHAPTER 8

MAKING HARDWICK HOME

In 1918, on the eleventh hour of the eleventh day of the eleventh month, the war was declared over. After four years and four months the guns fell silent. Celebrations erupted all over the country, from Trafalgar Square to the gardener's bothy at Clumber. I was pleased the war had come to an end, of course, but my heart was heavy with the loss of my family.

Work for the Women's Land Army was far from over, however. Even at peace, the country was low on supplies and it was some time before men started returning home. There was a real sense that things would never go back to the way they were before the war, and in lots of ways that was a good thing. Women were being asked to stay on in roles they had undertaken during the war effort. For the first time in history, women were being seen in a different light.

I had, for some time, decided to stay on at Clumber in any capacity I possibly could. Of course, my heart lay within the Walled Kitchen Garden but I understood clearly it was seen as a man's profession. However, in a tragic twist of fate, the young gardeners who went to war never returned to the soil of Clumber. It was Mr Barker himself who asked if I would like to stay on to work in the glasshouse. I didn't hesitate in telling him it would be an absolute honour. Mr Dawes was delighted and invited me to go and live with him and his wife in the village of Hardwick next to Home Farm. I was over the moon!

Gradually, one by one, the Land Girls of the Clumber Estate

returned to their lives around the country. Fond farewells and promises of letters were made. Sissy and James married in the church behind the big house with kind permission from the Duke and Duchess. Sissy made a beautiful bride; a dress of white lace showing that natural elegance I had noticed the first time I met her. The girls all returned for the big day and we gave them an arch of pitchforks to walk under as they left the church husband and wife. James and Sissy also settled in Hardwick; it was wonderful to have my best friend so close.

The Walled Kitchen Garden was as productive as ever and, in my opinion, was the magnificent jewel in the Clumber crown. I worked long days and loved every single minute. I stuck to my routine of watching the sun set and rise, painting the garden with unique colours and shades. It was one such evening I sat on the glasshouse steps and looked out at the garden changing before me. I took a deep breath of the dusk air and listened with my eyes closed as the birdsong began to quiet. It was then my ears heard the sound of uneven footsteps in the distance and my eyes opened to search out their source. Coming up the Ducal Walk was a man in uniform, walking with a cane. For a moment I thought it must be an acquaintance of the Duke and Duchess but as the figure drew closer, my heart started to hammer in my chest.

I slowly rose from the steps and in disbelief my feet started to move. Faster and faster they took me along the long range borders down to the gates. There he was before me, wearing his uniform and a smile I could never not recognise.

"Teddy?" I whispered and I ran into his arms before he could answer.

"I'm home," he said softly into my hair.

"Yes. Yes you are."

AFTERWORD

This work of fiction is based in historical fact. 100 years ago the Women's Land Army was formed and a training school was set up for ten young women to attend on the Clumber Estate. The Duke and Duchess of Newcastle agreed to pay for a housekeeper and maid for the duration and billeted them above the stables. You can walk around that very stable yard today and enjoy the shop and cafe. Home Farm in Hardwick Village is now no longer working but it was under the guiding hand of Mr Davey and you can still peek over the gate and see where the girls would have milked the cows. In Hardwick Village you will see the War Memorial where the names of farm hands and gardeners that never returned to Clumber are inscribed. The house no longer remains but you can explore the walled kitchen garden as it would have been in Clara's time. The Head Gardener at the time was indeed Mr Samuel Barker and you can enjoy an afternoon tea in what would have been his house. Unfortunately, the events at Poplar were also based in historical fact and a bomb was dropped through the school that fateful June day killing 18 children.

This story is dedicated to the women of the Women's Land Army, formed 100 years ago in 1917. "God speed the plough and the woman that drives it."

LESLEY MIDDLETON

GUILT OF THE INNOCENT

2ND PRIZE

For a long time, Lesley has been intrigued by the raw emotions and deeply-felt loyalties within mining communities.

In 1984, splits between family members in some parts of North Nottinghamshire, who disagreed on the issue of striking, had a devastating impact in some cases.

Lesley wanted to consider how actions taken at that time might affect relationships in those communities today.

She writes mostly short stories and flash fiction, purely as a hobby, although sometimes it seems to take over her life!

GUILT OF THE INNOCENT

Will Redman paid the driver and watched the taxi leave the car park. He'd hoped to slip in unnoticed at the last moment, but had miscalculated how long the journey would take. It had been a snap decision to come here today and already he was regretting it. He looked at the people traipsing across the car park – all strangers to him now.

Voices fell silent as the funeral procession arrived. Will strode the few steps to the building and joined the end of the line of mourners. All the seats were taken, so he stood behind the back row. But he wasn't the last to arrive. A well-dressed blonde woman ran through the doors just as they were closing and stood at his side. They acknowledged each other with a nod and joined in the singing of the first hymn, sharing the order of service that Will had been given as he came in.

After so long away, Will's mind started to wander. Thirty-two years: no wonder he didn't recognise any of the people here. He hoped they wouldn't recognise him either.

"I'm Clare," said the woman who had been standing beside him as they emerged into the fresh air. "Thank you for letting me share your hymn sheet."

"No worries," he muttered. There was an awkward pause. "My name's Will." He hadn't intended to tell her his name, but it felt rude not to. He certainly didn't intend to divulge any other information.

"Are you going to the wake?" asked Clare.

"No. I've no transport."

"No problem. I'll give you a lift."

"No need. Thank you all the same." The last thing Will wanted was having to converse with people from his past, people who might still bear him a grudge.

"Please come," Clare pleaded. "I won't know anyone there and it's important that I go. I'd be very grateful for your company. My car's just over there." She pointed to a tiny white Fiat parked in a space marked 'Staff Only'.

"Do you work here?" he asked.

"No." Clare laughed. "It was the only vacant space when I arrived – late as usual!"

"Why is it so important for you to go to the wake if you don't know people?" Will asked as they approached the car.

"I'm a journalist," said Clare. "I'm writing a piece on how the Sherwood and Dukeries area has changed since the pits closed. I wanted to interview Jim Breedon, but he was too ill and then, when he died, I thought I'd come and pay my respects. Jim had quite a following amongst the striking miners in 1984."

Will said nothing. Another awkward silence.

"How did you know him?" Clare persisted.

Will gave a deep sigh. He really didn't want to say any more.

Clare glanced across at him.

"Jim Breedon was my uncle."

"That's a bit of a let-down. I was expecting something much more sinister than that," said Clare. "So was there some history between you and Jim; did you not get on?"

Will cringed inwardly. Were all journalists this nosy or was Clare exceptionally inquisitive?

"I'm not going to tell you anything that you can put in a story," he said firmly.

"Fair enough. Off the record then." She hoped Will wouldn't notice that she'd crossed her fingers as she was speaking.

"Do you remember the miners' strike in 1984?" Will asked.

"Vaguely. My dad was one of the managers in the pits at that time."

"Well, you'd better keep that to yourself when we get to the wake," said Will. "Jim and his son were on strike, as, I suspect, were most of the people who'll be there."

"Were you?" asked Clare.

"No. Nor was me dad," he said, slipping into the local dialect as he thought back in time.

"Is that why you didn't want to come to the wake?"

He shrugged. "Loyalties and grievances last a long time in pit communities. If anyone recognises me things could get nasty."

"How long is it since you were here?" Clare asked.

"I left in December 1984 after a blazing row with Jim."

"About not striking?"

"Yes. Dad wouldn't strike. He stuck it out – carried on working despite all the aggro. I'd told him I were going to join the strike and he were gutted. Felt I'd betrayed him. I felt terrible. Any road, seeing Uncle Jim and me dad – his own brother-in-law – arguing like that just pushed me over the edge. I packed me things and left that night. And I've never been back."

"Do you realise your local accent's come back, Will? I thought you were an Aussie when I first met you but now you're talking just like a local."

"I am a local. And proud of it." Will paused. "Although I'm not proud of running away to Australia when the going got tough."

"How old were you?"

"Eighteen."

"Couldn't handle the pressure, I suppose. No-one could blame you for that," said Clare as she pulled into the crowded pub car park in Wellow.

"Hang on a minute, Clare," said Will as she opened the car door. "You're sure you want to do this? It could get unpleasant for both of us."

"I've got to. I need to get some material for my article. Tell you what, we'll give it an hour and then I'll take you wherever you want to go."

"Okay." Reluctantly, Will got out of the car. "I'll go and get us some drinks. What do you want?"

"Just soda water please." Clare led the way into the pub and disappeared amongst the crowd.

Will picked up the drinks from the bar. As he turned, he recognised the woman next to him. He tried to remember her name; she'd been dating Jim's son at the time of the strike. Linda – that was it. This was just what he'd dreaded.

"Well, look what's crawled in!" Will cringed at Linda's loud, high-pitched voice. "I do believe it's Will Redman. After all this time. Daring to show 'is face 'ere again."

Linda climbed up onto a stool.

"Listen, everyone. I've got something to say," Linda shouted. The barman obligingly rang the bell to get everyone's attention.

The room fell silent as Linda pointed her finger at Will. He had a drink in each hand and was surrounded by hostile faces. He felt his colour rising. If this turned nasty he had no means of defending himself.

"This man here is Will Redman. For those of you who are too young to remember, he were a scab, like his dad, Les. Now what we wanna know, mister scab, is what tha's doing here at Jim's funeral. Has tha' no respect?"

A muttering filtered through the crowded room. Someone jostled Will and he spilt some of Clare's soda water on the shoes of a man in front of him.

"'Hey watch it, scab." The man raised his fist.

"Sorry, mate." Will muttered. "Can I just get past please?"

"Is tha' going?" called Linda as Will edged his way past the man. "Good riddance. Let him go, Trev."

Belatedly Will recognised the man whose shoes he'd soaked. It was Trevor, Jim's son. As boys he and Trev had been best mates but the strike had changed everything. They'd had a punch-up over it and had avoided each other after that.

Reluctantly the crowd parted to let Will through. As he got outside, he placed the drinks on one of the tables, relieved the animosity towards him hadn't been even worse.

He was thankful it was too cold for most people to want to sit outside – even the smokers. None of his former friends and neighbours had followed him out. He hoped Clare wouldn't experience the sort of hostility that had been directed at him. It had been a mistake to come here today.

***

"Presumably you didn't let on who you were," said Will when Clare eventually emerged unscathed from the pub.

"No. They might have twigged if I used my maiden name," said Clare, pulling her coat tighter to keep out the cold.

"You're married then?" asked Will.

"Divorced."

"Children?"

"No." Clare paused. "You?"

"No to both." Will stood up. "Can we go now?"

"Sure. Where are we going?" Clare asked as they strode across to the car.

"I'm booked into a hotel in Edwinstowe. The Dukeries Lodge – you know it?"

"I know where it is," said Clare. "Do they do meals?"

"I hope so. I haven't had anything since breakfast."

"In that case, I'll buy you dinner, on expenses. It's the least I can do having put you through all that unpleasantness," said Clare.

"There's no need. If you just drop me off that'll be fine." The last thing Will wanted was more of Clare's questions.

"No. I insist," said Clare. "I hate eating on my own." She went to the bar to order their food.

This had been a favourite venue for Will's family's birthday and anniversary celebrations. His happy childhood memories were why he'd decided to book a room at the hotel. His recollections were interrupted as Clare placed their drinks on the table.

"My turn for a grilling now is it?" he asked.

"I promised you anything you said would be off the record." She held up her hands. "And I haven't got my fingers crossed this time."

"Did you get what you needed at the wake?" asked Will.

Clare took a sip of her drink. "Mostly, although there is something I want to ask you about."

"What?"

"Who's Rob Cowell?"

"Why do you want to know about him?" he asked.

"People were talking about him. Someone said they shouldn't have been so quick to throw you out; that they should have asked you about Rob Cowell."

"Why would they want to ask me about Rob Cowell?"

"I asked one of the men that," said Clare. "He said Rob left at the same time you did. Until today nobody had heard anything from either of you and you might know where Rob is. Is he a relative of yours?"

"He was Jim's foster son. He were only fourteen. Always seemed a bit lost really – hung about on his own a lot, skipped school, that sort of thing. Had a kind heart, though." Will was once again slipping back into the local vernacular as his memories were stirred.

"When did you last see him?"

"The night I left. I were round at Jim's house with Mum and Dad. I'd just told Jim I was going to join the strikers but Dad and Jim were arguing 'cos Dad said he was carrying on working. Rob came in. He were very pleased with himself. He'd stolen some money from one of the managers' houses. Jim were livid. I can remember exactly what he said. 'Tha' stupid little tyke. We mebbe 'ard up but we i'nt thieves.' I could see the hurt on Rob's face. It sickened me. I went home, packed me stuff and left."

"Where did you go?"

"I hitched down to London. Then I met a guy in a pub who said they were looking for miners in Australia. So that's where I went."

"Hence the Aussie accent," Clare commented. "Well, Notts-Aussie! Is this the first time you've been back?"

Will nodded and picked up his glass.

"You going back to Australia?" Clare asked.

"Yep. Sooner the better really. I'd forgotten how cold it gets here."

"Did you come back specially for Jim's funeral?"

"No. I got word that me mum's in a bad way."

"What's wrong with her?" Clare asked.

"Terminal cancer and dementia. She's in a home in Worksop. I've come over to clear out her house. It's got to be sold to pay her care home fees."

"What about your dad?"

"He died some years back."

"And you didn't come to his funeral?"

"I didn't know about it until it were too late."

"How did you know about Jim's funeral?"

"I saw the obituary in this morning's Worksop Guardian. It were a spur of the moment thing."

To Will's relief, their food arrived. He'd told Clare more about himself and his family than he'd ever told anyone else. She'd certainly got a knack of getting him to talk, whether he wanted to or not.

***

Clare arrived at Will's hotel just before nine-thirty the next morning. She'd managed to persuade Will to let her drive him to his mother's care home. Her journalistic instincts told her that there was still more of Will's story to be unearthed. Anyway, it was Saturday and she'd not much else planned for her day.

"Tell me about you," said Will as they drove past the outskirts of Sherwood Forest. He was determined not to let Clare delve further into his life history. "How did you become a journalist?"

"I did some work experience at a local paper when I was at school. I loved it. They gave me a job when I finished my A levels."

"Have you worked for any of the national papers?" asked Will.

"Only freelance. I'm doing this story for one of the Sunday papers. That's why I didn't want to miss the chance to talk to people at Jim's wake."

"Can you make a living as a freelance?" asked Will.

"I wish!" Clare laughed cynically. "I also work for a free local magazine based in Sheffield."

"Do you live in Sheffield?"

"No. Worksop. Quite near here." Clare said as she pulled into the care home's car park. "Can I come in with you?" she asked. "It's freezing out here."

Will opened his mouth to object but it was too late: she was already several paces ahead of him.

"I don't know if she'll recognise you," said the manager as she escorted them to Will's mother's room. "She gets a bit confused sometimes." She pushed the door open. "Doreen, you've got some visitors."

"Hello, Mum." Will took his mother's hand as her tired eyes scrutinised his face. "It's Will, Mum. I've come back."

"Will?" The old woman looked perplexed. "Tha's not my Will. Tha's too old. My Will's nobbut a lad."

"It is me, Mum." Will perched on the bed. "I've been away too long. I'm sorry. I should have come back sooner."

Doreen looked past Will. "Who's this?"

"Hello, Mrs Redman. I'm Clare, a friend of Will's."

"Come and sit down, me duck," she said, pointing at a chair by the bed. "I don't bite." Doreen turned back to Will. "Well, lad. Where's tha bin all these years?"

Will gave her a potted history of his time in Australia. Clare listened intently but was disappointed to discover that he seemed to have lived a very uneventful life out there.

"Can I ask you a question, Mrs Redman?" said Clare.

"Of course, dear," said Doreen.

"What happened to Rob Cowell?"

Doreen gasped. "Who?" The blood seemed to have drained from her face. The old lady took a deep breath and closed her eyes.

Will looked sharply at Clare. "Perhaps we'd better go," he said. "I'll come back and see you another day, Mum."

There was no reply from his mother. Thinking she'd fallen asleep, Will and Clare left her room on tiptoe.

Half an hour later, Will collected the keys to Doreen's house from the estate agent handling the sale. Will said he would take a bus to Ollerton but Clare insisted that she had nothing else to do and would drive him.

Clare's instincts were on high-alert again. Doreen's reaction to her question about Rob had been interesting. There was a mystery there and Clare was determined to get to the bottom of it.

***

"It's the one with the 'For Sale' board outside," said Will as they approached his mother's house.

"I'll leave you here for a bit," said Clare, to Will's relief. "I'm going to see if I can find Constable Wetherby."

"Who's he?"

"He was a local bobby when I lived here. He'll no doubt have retired by now but he might still be around. And he might give me some quotes for my article."

As Will stepped back from the car, he was approached by a couple with a dog. Clare looked back as she turned the corner and saw them walking towards Doreen's house.

She parked her car on the street where she and her parents had lived. There was a pub a few doors away. There might be someone there who knew where Constable Wetherby was living now. Fewer than half a dozen people were in the bar. Their conversations stopped as she walked in.

“What can I get you?” asked the landlord.

“Soda water, please. And whatever you’re having.”

“Thanks.” He started to pour Clare’s drink. “You new in these parts?”

“Not really,” said Clare. “I lived here until I was about ten.” She took a five pound note from her purse. “Maybe you can help me. I was hoping I might find Constable Wetherby.”

“Old Fred Wetherby! He retired years ago. What’s tha’ want him for?”

“I’m a journalist. I’m writing a piece about Ollerton. I was hoping he might be able to clarify a few points for me.”

“Well, lass, tha’ might be in luck. He usually comes in ‘ere on a Saturday.” He took a mouthful of beer. “What’s it to do with, then, this thing you’re writing about Ollerton?”

“How things have changed since the pits closed.”

“Huh. Not for the better, that’s for sure.” He looked towards the door as an elderly man came in. “Heyup, Fred. This lass is ‘ere to see thee.”

“Constable Wetherby. How are you?” Clare introduced herself. She used her maiden name this time.

“I remember. You were that little lass what had her pendant stolen when someone broke in to your dad’s house.”

"Yes that's right," said Clare. "It was a birthday present."

"Aye. Whoever took that stole three hundred pounds from your Mum's kitchen drawer and picked up your pendant on his way out. We never got him. We had a suspect but he disappeared."

"It wasn't Rob Cowell by any chance?" suggested Clare.

Fred Wetherby nodded. "Strange business that. Those were bad times. Families at each other's throats, police being bussed in to try and keep order. And the poverty. Some of the striking families had no fuel, no food, nothing."

"Let me get you a drink," said Clare.

They sat at a table near the fire. Two other men were sitting nearby.

"What can you tell me about Rob Cowell?" asked Clare.

"What's tha wantin' to know about him for?" It was one of the men at a neighbouring table who spoke.

"Go on, Billy. Tell us what tha' knows," said Fred.

"'E lived at Jim Breedon's 'ouse, next door to me. 'E just disappeared. Same time as Jim's nephew."

"Was that Will Redman?" prompted Clare.

"Aye. Some people thought they'd gone together but I dunno. I saw young Will thumbing a lift at the side of the A614. I were going t'other way or I'd have picked him up. But I didn't see anyone with him."

"I never knew that," said Fred. "When we went to question Rob about the burglary, Jim told us Rob had left home and gone with Will. I wonder what did happen to Rob Cowell."

"Will Redman's back, Fred," said Billy. "'E were at Jim's funeral yesterday. Mebbe ‘e knows what happened to Rob.”

Clare thanked the men for their help and made her apologies. She needed to go to the supermarket. As she pushed her trolley around Tesco she tried to work out what questions to ask Will. All her instincts were telling her that he knew more about what had happened to Rob Cowell than he was telling.

***

As Clare approached Doreen’s house she could see a police car parked outside. The front door of the house opened and Will came out flanked by two uniformed police officers.

“Am I under arrest?” Will asked as they walked along the path.

“Why would you think that, sir?” The officer put his hand on Will’s head and pushed him into the back of the police car.

Clare watched as Will was driven off. A young policewoman was tying police tape between a lamp post and the garden fence to cordon off the area.

“Excuse me. Can you tell me what’s happening, please?” Clare called out.

“This is a crime scene. Kindly move on, madam,” the policewoman said, turning away. Clare walked back to her car.

In the next hour she watched as various police vehicles arrived. A small group of neighbours was gathering outside the taped-off area. She dug a notebook and a pen out of her bag and went across to the little cluster of people.

“What’s going on?” she asked one of the women.

“They’ve just arrested someone in Doreen’s house.”

“Who?” Clare asked.

"Will Redman," said a man standing next to her. "'E were at the funeral yesterday. I knew 'e were a wrong 'un."

"Why have they arrested him?" Clare persevered.

"They probably think 'e 'ad summat to do wi' that lad what went missing all them years ago."

A van pulled up next to them. The policewoman asked the onlookers to move out of the way. As the van doors opened Clare could see forensic equipment stacked in boxes. Two men began putting on plastic coveralls.

Clare had never been so close to a crime scene before. As a journalist she needed to find out as much as she could. She looked across at the houses each side of the cordoned-off area. If she could get one of those two householders to let her in she might get sight of the back of Doreen's house. She turned to the woman she'd spoken to before.

"Who lives there?" she asked pointing to the nearest house.

"I do," said the woman. "Why?"

"I'm a reporter," said Clare. "I need to get a better idea of what's going on. Any chance you'd let me have a look out of your back bedroom window?"

The woman looked doubtful.

"I'd like to interview you as well. You know, find out about the family."

The woman's expression softened.

"All right, then. I'll do it for Doreen."

"What's your name?" asked Clare.

"Debs. Debs Clark."

Clare introduced herself as she followed the woman into the house.

Upstairs, Clare and Debs edged round the double bed that took up most of the space and looked over into Doreen's garden. Several police officers were shovelling earth from what appeared to be a neglected vegetable patch onto the lawn. While they were watching, two men in protective suits erected a tent over the area being dug.

"Never mind, duck." Debs could see Clare's disappointment. "Come downstairs and have a cuppa. I'll tell thee what tha' needs to know – what I can, any road."

In the kitchen, Debs filled the kettle.

"Were you living here at the time of the '84 strike?" asked Clare.

"Aye. We moved in when we got married in '83. Les and Doreen were next door wi' Will. Les worked through the whole of the strike and there were some around here who never spoke to him again. But Doreen and me, we stayed mates. She's in a home now, though."

"Did you know Jim Breedon?" asked Clare.

"Aye – Doreen's brother. He lived three doors along the street. Hang on; didn't I see you at his funeral yesterday?"

"Yes," Clare admitted. "Do you remember the night that Will left home?"

"I do, because there were a lot of activity in Les and Doreen's back garden that night. I mentioned it to Doreen at the time and she said Les had been so angry and frustrated about the strike and an argument he'd had wi' Jim that he went out to dig the vegetable plot to try and calm himself down."

"Was Will with him?" Clare asked.

"I dunno. There were two men in the garden but I couldn't see who they were. It were dark. It might have been Will wi' 'is dad. I don't really know. But I never saw Will again after that."

"What about Rob Cowell?"

"'E lived wi' Jim; had done for several years. He were a nice lad in many ways but always hangin' around wi' nowt to do."

"What happened to him?"

"He left – same time as Will. Jim said Rob had gone wi' Will. Nobody heard 'owt from either of 'em 'til Will turned up at the funeral . . ." Debs stopped mid-sentence as shouts were heard from Doreen's garden next door. The two women quietly stepped out into Debs's back garden and positioned themselves close to the six-foot high fence.

"Yes, sir," they heard one of the policemen say. "It's definitely a human skeleton."

A horrified look appeared on Debs's face.

"I've got to go," Clare said. "Just quickly, though, what can you tell me about Doreen?"

"Doreen's lovely. Her hubby weren't striking but that didn't stop her helpin' the strikers' wives where she could. They put on a Christmas party for the kids that year. They were struggling to get enough money together and then a mystery donation suddenly came in: three hundred pounds!"

***

At the police station, Will was shown into an interview room. A man wearing civilian clothes followed him in.

"Perhaps you'll tell me." Will tried to keep his tone calm and measured. "Am I under arrest?"

"No, sir. You're here voluntarily to help us with our enquiries," the man said.

"What enquiries?"

"We'll get to that shortly, sir. First, though, I need your fingerprints and a sample of your DNA for elimination purposes."

Will shrugged and let the man do his job. When he'd finished Will asked again: "What enquiries do I need to be eliminated from?"

"The disappearance of Rob Cowell in 1984."

"Do I need a solicitor?" Will asked.

"I don't know. Do you?" As he left the room, the man smirked at Will.

The police seemed in no hurry to question Will. It was almost two hours before the door to the interview room opened and an older man in a dishevelled, mismatching jacket and trousers came in with the detective who'd taken Will's fingerprints. They sat across the table from Will. The more senior man switched the recording machine on and stated his name: Detective Chief Inspector John Murray. Then his colleague did the same: Detective Sergeant Pete Lucas. He asked Will to state his name and address for the tape.

"William Redman. I'm currently staying at the Dukeries Lodge hotel in Edwinstowe. Normally I live in Australia."

"Why have you come to the UK, Mr Redman? Or can I call you Will?" asked the older man.

"My mother is in a care home. I've got to sell her house to pay for her care."

The younger man read out an address in Ollerton. "Is that your mother's address?"

"Yes."

"What were you doing there today?"

"I've just told you. I went to start sorting things out ready to sell the house."

"Talk us through what happened at the house before our officers brought you here today."

"I'd just got to the house when a couple arrived asking if they could look round. They hadn't got an appointment or anything. They'd got a dog with them that had been rolling about in some muck in the fields. They put it in the back garden while I showed them round. They said they'd contact the estate agent if they wanted to make an offer. That's about it, really."

"Why were you digging in the back garden?"

"I wasn't. The dog had been digging in the vegetable patch. It had made a right mess! I was shovelling the earth back off the path, trying to tidy it up."

"When was the last time you saw Rob Cowell?" It was the older man who asked the question this time.

"It was 1984, at my Uncle Jim's house – Jim Breedon. He were Rob's foster father. Jim and my dad had a big row and then Rob came in and Jim started on him. I'd had enough. I walked out, packed a few things and went. Never saw any of them again."

"Was that the last time you were in the UK, Will?" DCI Murray asked.

"Yes."

"You see, that's what I'm finding difficult to understand. In thirty-two years you've never once been back to see your mother and father. Why's that?"

Will shrugged. "I don't know, really. When I left, things were very unpleasant. I had no great desire to come back."

"We've been told you were at Jim Breedon's funeral yesterday, Will." The younger man took up the questioning again.

"Yes. I was."

"I understand Jim's family weren't best pleased to see you. Why might that have been?"

"We were on opposite sides in the strike. They've never forgiven that."

There was a knock at the door. The older man stepped outside. DS Lucas switched off the tape, sat back and folded his arms. Will began to feel uncomfortable under the man's stare but he was determined not to be the one to break the silence.

"We'll find out, you know." DS Lucas said. "Sooner or later." He looked away as the door opened and DCI Murray beckoned to him. As they left the room, a uniformed officer entered and stood by the door.

"Stand up, please, Mr Redman," DS Lucas instructed as he and DCI Murray entered the room. Will glanced at his watch. He'd now been at the police station for over four hours.

Will did as he was told.

"William Redman, I am arresting you . . ."

Will was so shocked he couldn't take in any of the other words the police officer was saying. He was led to the custody suite and ordered to hand over his watch, empty his pockets and remove his belt. He'd never felt so humiliated in his life.

The police agreed to contact Clare to let her know that Will had been arrested. They kept him in a cell for what seemed like several hours before leading him back to the interview room. A duty solicitor was waiting there for him. She introduced herself as Lucy Firman. After a brief discussion, Lucy went to the door to tell the police officer outside that Will was ready to be interviewed.

As the police officers switched on the recording machine and went through the procedures necessary to identify everyone present, Will tried hard to pull himself out of the dazed stupor he felt himself sinking into.

"Do you recognise this, Will?" DCI Murray asked, pushing a clear plastic bag across the table which contained a small jewellery box. Smears of mud had soiled the polythene.

"I don't think so. Why?"

"What about this?" A second plastic bag was pushed across the table towards Will.

"I, er ..." He looked at his solicitor.

"It's a simple enough question, Will." DCI Murray's tone was impatient. "Do you recognise it or not?"

"It looks like a necklace or a pendant," said Will.

"Have you seen it before?"

"No," said Will.

"Then why are your fingerprints on these items?" DCI Murray sat back in his chair.

Will closed his eyes as suddenly every detail of the last time he'd seen Rob came back to him. "Rob showed me a necklace. I'd forgotten about it – it was only for a couple of seconds. He'd stolen it along with some money. A few hundred pounds, I think.

He thought he'd done good, getting some money and a nice bit of jewellery that could be sold. His family were very hard up – they'd been on strike for near on a year."

"Tell me again why you were digging in your mother's back garden, Will." The younger detective was speaking now. "Was it to remove anything that might implicate you in Rob Cowell's death before the house is sold?"

Will turned to his solicitor. This was starting to look very bad for him.

***

The police held Will in custody for twenty-four hours. They reluctantly let him go when his solicitor pointed out that they had nothing other than circumstantial evidence – and not very much of that. It was hardly surprising that Will wouldn't recognise a necklace he'd held for just a few seconds thirty-two years ago. And what would have been Will's motive in killing Rob?

Clare was waiting for him outside the police station.

"I feel really embarrassed about accepting so many favours from you," said Will, relieved to see her.

"Don't be daft. And anyway, I'm hoping I might get a juicy story out of this." She grinned at him. She was only half- joking.

"Tell me what happened," Clare said as they drove back to her house in Worksop.

"Apparently a neighbour of Mum's phoned the police when he looked out of his back bedroom window and thought he saw me digging up the garden. He'd been at Jim's wake and recognised me. Someone else who was at the wake had already told the police that I was back, and it seems they'd been wanting to ask me about Rob's disappearance ever since 1984. On the basis of what the neighbour said, they dug down in the garden themselves and found something."

"A skeleton?" Clare prompted. "It's been on the local news." She didn't tell Will that she'd been the one who'd given them the story.

"They seem to think it's Rob, and that I'd gone there to move the body before selling the house," Will continued. "Oh, and they also found a necklace."

"What sort of necklace?"

"A pendant. It had, like, two commas wrapped round each other."

"Yin and yang," murmured Clare. "I had one like that."

"Really?"

"I got it for my tenth birthday. It was stolen along with some money from our house. Perhaps I ought to tell the police. They don't take kindly to people withholding information," said Clare.

***

On Monday morning, Clare went into work. Will caught the bus to Worksop to see Doreen again. He was determined to get back to Australia as quickly as he could, and wanted to spend as much time as possible with his mother before he went.

Doreen's delight at seeing Will didn't last long. Within half an hour of his arrival, the manager showed DCI Murray and DS Lucas into his mother's room.

"These gentlemen are policemen, Doreen," she said.

Doreen's eyes filled with tears.

"'Ave you come for me?" she asked.

The two detectives looked at each other with surprise.

"I don't know, Mrs Redman. Should we have?"

"It were me that did it."

"Did what, Mrs Redman?"

"I'm not saying."

The more senior of the two officers looked across at Will. "Could we speak outside for a moment, please, Mr Redman?"

"We've just come to ask your mother if she can tell us what happened on the day Rob Cowell disappeared and what she knows about the money and the pendant. We don't want to cause her any distress. Is there anyone else we could talk to?"

"No. I've told you all I know. The only other people there were my dad and Jim Breedon, Mum's brother. They're both dead now."

"I see. Forgive me for asking, but is your mother, er, compos mentis?"

"She's very confused, I'm afraid. And she's very ill. I hope you're not going to question her in the same manner you questioned me."

The two police officers walked away and conferred together out of Will's hearing.

"We're quite happy for you to sit in while we talk to your mother, Mr Redman, if that would make it easier for her."

It was as Will feared. Even with him present, Doreen very quickly became distressed and the manager of the home insisted that the police desist from their questioning of her.

Later, at Clare's house with a takeaway curry and a bottle of wine,

Will recounted the conversation to her.

"They asked Mum what happened when Rob came in that night. She said she couldn't remember him being there. Then she started saying Jim wasn't there, either."

"But wouldn't you think she'd remember something like that? You said it was a furious row and most of the people you talk to about those times can remember just about everything that happened back then."

"She says she doesn't remember." Will shrugged.

His mobile phone rang.

"Yes." He paused to listen. "Right. Yes. I'll come straight away." He ended the call. "Mum's had a stroke. She's in a bad way."

"Come on. I'll take you in the car."

Seeing his mother lying against the pillows made Will regret the years he'd been away. The police were right to be critical of him; he hadn't been a good son and now it was too late to make things right. He sat down and took her hand.

"It's me, Mum. Will. I'm here now."

Doreen's lips moved, but he couldn't tell what she said. He bent his head closer.

" . . . Priest," was all he could make out.

He ran out to the car where Clare was waiting for him. "She wants a priest," he said to her.

"I'll get one."

"What do you want to confess, Mum?" Will said as he sat down by her bed again. "Can you tell me?"

Doreen opened her eyes and stared directly at her son. There was no recognition there.

"It were me. I put the bag on his head to catch the blood. He couldn't breathe. I'm sorry. Jim hit Rob but it were me that killed him."

"No, Mum. Don't say that. You didn't. It were an accident. Rob fell and hit his head on the table when Jim punched him. That's what killed him."

"No. When they picked him up to carry him outside, I heard him moan. He were still alive then."

"No, Mum. That would just be air escaping from his throat. He were already dead." Will was sure he'd read somewhere that such a thing could happen, and his Mum mustn't go to her grave thinking she'd killed Rob.

His mother fell back against the pillows, still holding Will's hand.

"Will. I've brought Father Michael." Clare and a priest were standing in the doorway.

Will hadn't realised there was anyone else in the room. He wondered how long they'd been there.

"Thank you for coming, Father." Will got up to greet the priest. "She thinks she killed someone called Rob. She didn't. Please do what you can to comfort her."

Will and Clare waited outside whilst the priest was with Doreen.

"How much did you hear?" Will asked Clare.

Clare drove Will back to his hotel in Edwinstowe.

"How can you be so sure that the blow to Rob's head was what killed him?" she asked.

Will hesitated momentarily.

"The police told me."

"But your mother seemed to think otherwise. And she was there."

Will said nothing.

"Oh, well, just a thought." Clare shrugged. "I'm off home. I'll call you in the morning."

***

After a sleepless night Will decided it was the turn of the police to answer his questions. DCI Murray and DS Lucas were already busy when he got to the police station, and he knew he could have a long wait. So be it. He couldn't have his mother going to her grave convinced that she'd been the one who'd killed Rob.

There was only one thing on his mind. What had killed Rob that day?

"Thank you for coming in, Clare." It was DS Lucas's voice. Will turned to see him shaking hands with Clare.

"Clare? What are you doing here?" he asked.

"Sorry to keep you waiting, Mr Redman," DS Lucas interrupted. "We'll be with you in a few minutes."

Clare sat down next to Will.

"They asked me to come in and have a look at the pendant – to see if it was mine. It was. I've just been giving them a statement. Why are you here?"

"I want to get to the bottom of what killed Rob. I can't stop thinking about what Mum said about the plastic bag."

As Clare left to go to work, DS Lucas came to escort Will to the same interview room he'd been in before.

"I need to know what caused Rob's death," Will said, as assertively as he could.

"According to the pathologist it was a head wound." DCI Murray paused. "Why?"

Will ignored the question.

"How can you be so certain when there's only a skeleton for the pathologist to examine? What if it had been something else, like suffocation?"

"What makes you think he might have been suffocated, Will?" asked DS Lucas.

"Or stabbed, or poisoned, or drowned," Will said quickly, realising his error. "For example."

The two detectives looked steadily at him.

"How can you even be sure it's Rob?" Will asked.

"Dental records," said DCI Murray. He stood up. "Excuse us a minute, Will." He and DS Lucas left the room.

Will began to wish he'd left things as they were. His instinct was to get back to Australia on the first available plane. But he certainly couldn't let his mother take the blame for Rob's death. When the two detectives returned to the room and sat down, DCI Murray was carrying a folder. He opened it and took out a couple of sheets of paper.

"I hope you've got a strong stomach, Will," he said, pushing one of the pages towards him. It was a photo of a partially skeletonised head, showing the location and dimensions of an injury. He gave Will chance to study the image and then pushed a second page across the table.

"Read that," he said, pointing to a paragraph near the end of the page.

Will found the technical terminology difficult to understand but the final sentence was clear enough. 'Death would have been instantaneous.'

"Does that answer your question, Will?" asked DCI Murray.

Will nodded. He started to get up but DCI Murray continued.

"There was a plastic bag tied over the head. We think whoever moved the body perhaps did that so they wouldn't get covered in blood. But the pathologist says it was the blow to the head that killed Rob. No doubt about it. It seems Rob had an unusually thin skull."

"It's a shame your mother can't remember who was there that night," said DS Lucas, fixing Will with an accusatory look.

***

Clare phoned Will as soon as she got home that evening. "Everything OK?" she asked.

"The postmortem report says Rob died as a result of a head injury."

"So your Mum's in the clear then?"

"Yes."

"What now?" asked Clare.

"I'm coming over to Worksop to tell her."

"Come and have a meal with me after."

"Thanks," said Will. "I'll bring some wine."

His mother was asleep when he arrived. He sat holding her hand, reflecting on the agonies she must have gone through, believing she'd killed Rob.

As she opened her eyes, a tear ran down her cheek. He passed her a tissue from the box by the bed.

"I'm sorry, Will."

"You've nothing to be sorry about, Mum. Rob died when his head hit the table. The police are quite clear about that. I've seen the pathologist's report."

"But we were there. If we'd called an ambulance, Rob might have lived."

"No, Mum. The report said he had an unusually thin skull. He died as soon as he hit his head."

Doreen smiled at him and closed her eyes.

It was half an hour before Will realised she'd stopped breathing.

"What are you going to do now?" Clare asked as she washed up the dishes.

Will took a soapy plate from her and wiped it on a tea towel.

"I'm going to move into Mum's house until it's sold."

"You're not going back to Australia, then?"

"Not for a bit, anyway."

"What I can't understand," said Clare, "is why Rob was buried in your parents' garden when the row took place at Jim's house."

Will felt himself go cold. He'd been right about Clare's journalistic instincts.

"Jim's back yard had been concreted over."

"So Jim and Les carried Rob's body along the street?"

"No. All those houses back onto a field. They went that way."

"You were there when it happened?" Clare sounded incredulous. "Tell me about it."

Will finally relented. There was no other way to stop Clare's questions.

"Rob came in and threw the cash onto the coffee table," he began. "He handed me a small blue box."

***

"Open it," Rob said as Will hesitated.

Will lifted a silver pendant out of the box.

"Where'd you get this?" he asked, thrusting the necklace and box back at Rob.

"Same place as the dosh. Good, eh?"

Will looked across at his uncle. Jim had a reputation for being very free with his fists.

Jim pushed past Will. 'Tha' stupid little tyke. We mebbe 'ard up but we i'nt thieves.' He punched Rob's chin hard and Rob fell backwards, hitting his head on the coffee table.

"No!" Will was already at Rob's side. Blood was trickling from a wound on the back of Rob's head. Will felt Rob's wrist for a pulse.

"Let me see." Les Redman bent down, his cheek against Rob's lips.

"What have you done, Jim?" Doreen wailed. "How could you do that to the lad?"

"He's dead, Jim," said Les, his face ashen.

"I'll call an ambulance," said Will. "I expect the police will come as well."

"No." Jim snatched the phone from Will's hand. "It were an accident."

"It were no accident. You killed him," said Doreen.

"With my record, I'll be sent down for years," pleaded Jim. "That's not going to bring him back. And the publicity will do no end of harm."

"I agree," said Les. "Let's just bury him. Best to say nowt about it."

"We can't do it 'ere. If we dig up the concrete it'll make a right racket."

"You're right, Jim. We'll put him in the veg patch at our house." Les looked again at the wound on Rob's head. "Best get summat to catch the blood, Doreen."

***

"So that's when I tied the bag round his head," said Will. "Jim and Dad carried Rob along the edge of the field and buried him in Dad's vegetable patch. When I saw that dog digging there on Saturday I knew we'd be found out."

Clare's face was impassive.

"Are you shocked?" Will asked her.

"Yes, I suppose I am," she said.

"Dad was certain Rob were dead as soon as he'd hit his head. Neither of us could feel a pulse. But, if he were still alive when I tied that plastic bag over his head, it would have been me that killed him," said Will. "I've spent the last thirty-two years trying to justify to myself not making that phone call, but I've never been able to. I should have gone ahead and told the police."

"You were only a lad," said Clare. "And with your dad and your uncle against you it would have been a difficult thing to do."

"I mean I should have told them today, when I was at the police station."

"What good would that do?" asked Clare. "The man responsible for Rob's death is dead. So is your dad and now your mum. The police would probably charge you with something like failing to report a death or perverting the course of justice and then you'd be the one sent to jail."

"Maybe that's what I deserve."

"That's what Jim deserved," said Clare. "But not you. You weren't to blame."

But Will knew the guilt would punish him for the rest of his life unless he atoned for what he did.

First thing in the morning, he'd go and see DCI Murray. It was time to lay the past to rest.

END

PAMELA MANN

THE DEATH OF ROBIN HOOD

3RD PRIZE

As a member of Bassetlaw Writers' Group, I have had a number of articles published over the years, as well as a children's picture book, and won many awards for my poetry, but never anything for my stories.

So I was thrilled to be told I had won 3rd prize in this competition. At seventy-one years of age, I can only conclude that you're never too old to fulfil an ambition.

I am grateful to the organisers of North Notts Short Story Competition for giving me a chance to show what I can do.

The idea for a murder mystery set in North Notts had long been in my mind and this year seemed a good time to finally get it written down. The victim had to be Robin Hood, our local hero, of course; but if not the man himself, at least someone wearing his clothes and using his name. So, determining the victim's true identity is the first piece of the puzzle that needs to be solved. *The Death of Robin Hood* is the result.

I'm a fan of murder mysteries and have read everyone from Agatha Christie to Retford's own Stephen Booth. I must say I never knew that writing one would such great fun.

Of course, I hope to enter the competition next year. Maybe I'll do even better next time around.

THE DEATH OF ROBIN HOOD

It was no day to be finding dead bodies. That's what was going through Luke's mind as he stumbled back home through the pouring rain. It was no day for walking an obstinate spaniel, either, but he'd foolishly agreed to help out more in exchange for an increase in his pocket money. If only he'd kept Sally away from the water. If only he'd gone in the opposite direction. If only...

The call to Nottinghamshire police was logged at 7.37 a.m. Detective Constable Joe (Tubby) Dale was sent to investigate at 7.50. The overweight D.C. was not best pleased at missing breakfast, let alone going in the rain to find what he felt sure would turn out to be a prank. A man dressed in Lincoln green and wearing tights found dead in Clumber Park close to the weir? They were pulling his leg, surely. If only...

Detective Inspector Ian Valiant from Worksop was heading up the investigation. He called his team together for a briefing at 9.30. A tall, good-looking man of forty-one, whose hair was beginning to thin on top, he had a habit of raising his heels off the ground whenever he was nervous or worried. He was doing it now.

"Right, Dale," he said. "What have you got for us? Do we have any I.D. for the victim?"

A titter went up from his assembled colleagues.

"Did I say something funny?"

Dale stood. "No, sir, it's just that the deceased, a man

of about thirty, was wearing an outfit of Lincoln green, including tights, so, naturally, everyone is calling him Robin Hood."

"Did he have anything on him?" asked Valiant.

Another titter.

"Just a quiver full of arrows, sir."

"I hope you're not winding me up, Dale."

Dale shook his head. "He was found by a lad, walking his dog first thing. Luke Enright, aged fourteen, from Hardwick Village."

"In Clumber? At that hour?"

"Hardwick village is in Clumber Park, sir. Easy walking distance to the weir."

"Is Enright a suspect?"

"No, sir. He was pretty cut up about finding the body. His parents are keeping him off school today if we should want to interview him again."

Ian Valiant began raising his heels.

"Not much to go on," he admitted. "What do you suppose Robin Hood was doing in Clumber? Re-enacting the fight scene with Little John?"

More tittering from the assembled officers, but this time the inspector knew he'd made a joke.

He continued. "We shan't know how he died until after the post mortem. How did he get into the park? Anyone looking for a vehicle?"

"Uniforms are scouring the park as we speak," Dale replied, "although it may take a while. There are two camping sites in the park so plenty of vehicles to check on."

Detective Sergeant Angela Scott raised her hand. In her late twenties and blonde, she would have been very pretty but for a port- wine birthmark which covered part of one cheek and ear.

Valiant turned on what he considered his most charming smile.

"He could have been to a fancy dress party, sir," Scott suggested. "We ought to check that angle, perhaps."

"Best idea I've heard all day. Well done, Angela. Get onto it will you. I've a post mortem to attend."

At four that afternoon, Valiant called in his detectives once again. The postmortem had puzzled him. Robin Hood had two wounds: a blow to the head with a blunt instrument, and a piercing through his heart with a sharp, pointed object. Either one would have killed him. The inspector needed to know who the man was so he could learn about his lifestyle and associates. Was he involved in criminal activity – drugs, for instance?

"Any news on a vehicle, Dale?" he asked.

"Nothing yet, sir. Uniforms are still making enquiries, but the security firm which checks the park at night haven't reported seeing anything suspicious. Unless he came with his assailant, he or she must have driven his car away."

"Nothing suspicious? A man lay dead and it wasn't suspicious?"

"To be fair, they're only required to check the park by van, sir. I had to walk to the point where the body was found."

"I suppose Hardwick Village isn't missing a resident?"

"No, sir."

Then DS Scott piped up. "Surely he couldn't have been home, otherwise he would have changed out of his outfit, wouldn't he?"

"Never," said Valiant, raising his heels, "underestimate the strange behaviour of the human race. Anything to report on the fancy dress angle?"

"Yes, sir. There was a party last night at the Clumber Park Hotel."

Valiant gave her a glowing smile. "Wonderful, Angela. Was our Robin Hood a resident?"

Angela Scott combed down one side of her lopsided hair so it covered her birthmark, before deflating the inspector's balloon.

"Only six of the partygoers were, I'm afraid. The party was some sort of charity do,

a gathering of local business people to raise money for the Hospice."

"And I don't suppose you're going to make my day by saying they had a list of all the people who attended this charity bash?"

"No, sir," she replied, "but of those who stayed overnight, one of them was a name you'll recognise. Cornelius Ryan."

Valiant's heels went up again. "I was hoping for the name of an ex-con, not the upright and immovable Mr Ryan, solicitor and magistrate of this town."

Scott continued. "One of the waiting staff said there were two Robin Hoods there last night but she couldn't say who they were."

"Two Robin Hoods!" cried an exasperated Valiant. "Oh, the joys of living in Nottinghamshire!"

"I've got the names of a couple of fancy dress shops, including one called Fancy Pants in Retford," Angela Scott went on. "I was hoping to check them out tomorrow to see if they'd hired a Robin Hood outfit to anybody, especially one who hadn't brought it back."

"Good idea," said the Inspector. "And I'll go and see Cornelius Ryan at his home.

Dale?"

"Sir?"

"You're with me."

Valiant and Dale were driving down the A60 heading for Southoaks, where the splendid home of Cornelius Ryan was situated. It wasn't long before a tailback of traffic

told them there was a tractor on the road ahead. To take the inspector's mind off the 15 miles per hour speed he was forced to endure, Dale asked him about Ryan.

"You said he was upright and immovable. Why?"

"Have you ever had to ask him for a search warrant to go through some toe rag's possessions?"

"Can't say as I have, sir."

"You will," Valiant assured him. "And when you do, be sure you've got a cast-iron, double-padlocked, waterproof reason for suspecting said toe rag, or you'll not get your warrant. We expect our magistrates to be upright but also reasonable. Cornelius Ryan isn't."

"Must be his legal training, sir."

"Maybe. But he doesn't handle criminal cases in his practice because he sits on the bench. Can't act for the defence. Conflict of interest, see?"

Before Dale had a chance to reply, Valiant turned his Peugeot off the main road down a country lane, its verges made more lush by recent rainfall. Another right turn and they were pulling up at the magnificent front door of Aysgarth Cottage, where Cornelius Ryan lived. Detached and set in grounds of about half an acre, the image it presented to the world was that of a successful and well-heeled man.

'Some cottage,' thought D.C. Dale.

The door was opened by an attractive woman of middle age, wearing a dressing gown and with a towel wrapped around her head. "Yes," she said rather abruptly. "What do you want?"

"Detective Inspector Valiant and Constable Dale," said Valiant as they showed their

warrant cards. "Is Mr Ryan at home?"

"Who is it, Betty?" asked a man's voice from within. A door opened and there stood

an impressive man, late sixties, tall and slim with a full head of grey hair. He was much older than Valiant but taller and with more hair.

"Oh, I know you, don't I? Inspector Intrepid, isn't it?" Ryan offered his hand, which Valiant reluctantly shook.

"Valiant, sir. D.I. Valiant."

"Yes, of course. Knew it was one of those blasted warships."

He took them into a spacious, airy conservatory overlooking an extensive garden. The roses were looking a bit bedraggled but the lawns were immaculate. Betty drifted away into another part of the house.

"Search warrant, is it?" asked Ryan. "Do take a pew."

The two officers sat on a luxurious, wicker sofa, well padded with cushions. A glass-topped wicker table stood between them and Mr Ryan.

"No, sir. We're making enquiries about an incident that happened last night in Clumber Park. We believe that the man who died had been to a fancy dress party. I believe you were at such a party last evening."

"Yes. Fundraiser for the Hospice. Of course, I didn't go in fancy dress myself. Can't retain suitable respect by prancing around as Napoleon or an Indian Chief. What's the fellow called?"

"That's just it, sir. We don't know yet and thought you might be able to help us. This is a photograph of the man. It was taken after death, so it's not very flattering."

Ryan studied the photograph. "Looks like Robin Hood," he joked. "That's the costume, of course. Now, I seem to recall there were two Robin Hoods at the party last night. One was a young farmer, good county stock. Name of Greenhalgh, Bobby Greenhalgh."

"Is this him?"

"No," said Ryan, giving the photo back to Valiant. "I don't know this chap at all."

"But he was at your party!"

"Not my party. I was just a guest, same as this fellow. The organiser was that doctor chappie from Tuxford. Eagle, that's his name. Doctor Eagle."

Dale, who'd been making not very copious notes, turned to leave, but Valiant hung back. "Were there any people carrying sharp knives at your... sorry, the party?"

"I don't know about sharp knives. Those costumes are only make-believe, you know." Ryan laughed. "There was someone dressed as a Scotsman. He'd a dirk in his sock. That the kind of thing?"

"Exactly. Take this down, Dale."

Ryan continued. "There was an Indian Chief. He may have had a dagger. Robin Hood had his arrows, of course. Couple of cowboys and a uniformed policeman, but they

wouldn't have anything like that. Doctor Eagle was a Cavalier, would you believe? He had a sword. Of course, in real life, a couple of them were surgeons. Access to all manner of sharp instruments."

'Oh, goody,' thought Valiant. 'This case has more angles than Pythagoras dreamed of.'

"Just how many people were at the party?" asked Valiant.

"Fifty, sixty at the most," replied Cornelius Ryan.

"So we've got sixty potential suspects?" Valiant sighed.

"Unless the attacker was someone who wasn't at the fancy dress party, Inspector. Have you considered that possibility?"

"I have considered all possibilities, sir," was Valiant's parting shot.

"Back to the station, sir?" asked Dale, whose stomach was beginning to rumble.

"I suppose so, but I'd have liked to identify Robin Hood before we finish for the day. Someone's reputation is on the line. Namely mine. You can drive."

Dale took the proffered keys in silence. The Inspector's mood was just about as gloomy as the weather.

As they covered the few miles to Worksop, Valiant asked "What did you make of Cornelius?"

Dale coughed. "He seemed pleasant enough. Getting a bit forgetful, though. He got your name wrong."

"That wasn't forgetfulness," Valiant said. "That was his way of getting the upper hand. Think yourself lucky he didn't call you Constable Hill."

"Was the woman, Betty, his wife? She's a lot younger than him."

"She's his second wife. The first one died, and before you jump to conclusions, it was cancer she died from. Betty came as a Nanny to his children while she was ill. Three

years later she married him. Of course, they were both much younger then. The boys must be quite grown up by now."

"What are your plans for tomorrow, sir?" Dale asked.

"A trip to Tuxford is well overdue. Let's see what Doctor Eagle has to say for himself. As soon as the morning briefing is out of the way, we'll head to his surgery."

At the early morning briefing, D.S. Scott had much to report. She'd caught Fancy Pants before they closed yesterday and had some success. One Robin Hood costume had been borrowed by a Robert Greenhalgh who'd returned it that morning. The other had gone to a Mr. Robin Hood.

"You're joking. Did he give an address?"

"An unlikely one, sir," Scott replied. "Green Trees, Sherwood Village, Forest Town."

"As you say, an unlikely one but check it out anyway. I'm off to meet the organiser of the fancy dress party, Doctor Eagle in Tuxford."

Angela was tempted to say that Eagle seemed an improbable name as well, but thought better of it.

By nine thirty Valiant and Dale were on the road for Tuxford. They hadn't got far when it began to rain again. Then Valiant's phone rang. It was the station. They'd had a complaint from the National Trust about part of the park being out of bounds to the public. They wanted to know how long it would be before it was opened up again. Valiant was tempted to say that it took as long as it took, but relented.

"Tell them we'll be out of there by tonight. Any clues will have been washed away in the deluge by now. But don't tell them that. O.K?"

He hung up, whereupon the phone immediately rang again.

"What now?" he yelled, but it was Angela Scott's voice on the line.

"I've just heard from another of the hotel staff, a part-timer who wasn't there at the original interview. She says she saw a fight between the two Robin Hoods. She didn't know what it was about but, it was stopped by a Cavalier who drew his sword and told them to stop it or he'd run them through."

"Really?" said Valiant. "How interesting. Well done, Angela."

Once they'd got past his receptionist and apologised for disrupting her schedule of patients, they found Doctor Eagle to be a jovial, middle-aged man, almost as round as Tubby Dale. He hadn't heard about the gruesome find in Clumber Park but was quite willing to provide the names and addresses of all the guests at the fancy dress party. He pulled them up on his computer screen and printed off a copy for the detectives.

"Could you tell us what outfits they were wearing?" asked Valiant. "We're particularly interested in the two Robin Hoods. We know one was Robert Greenhalgh but the other is a bit of a mystery."

"Ah, well," the doctor prevaricated, "I didn't really want him to be there as he wasn't quite one of us, but he asked me as a special favour." The doctor squirmed. "He said he'd give me a discount on my conservatory if I'd invite him to the party. He has a bit of a reputation, you see, with the ladies. Rumour has it that he's been discovered giving a few wives in the area more than just double glazing, if you get my drift."

"He got into a fight with Greenhalgh at the party. Was that over Mrs Greenhalgh?" Valiant probed.

The doctor said it probably was.

"A fight which you broke up by threatening to run them through with your sword. Is that what you did after the party? Get your double glazing fitter on his own and run him through?"

Doctor Eagle was shocked. "Absolutely not. I'm sworn to preserve life, not to destroy it. I told the men to keep their disagreements for outside. Reminded them that we were raising money for a charitable cause and didn't want to get a reputation for raucous behaviour. I may have jokingly said something about running them through, but I'd no intention of doing it. When the party broke up, I came home with my wife."

"What did she go as?" Dale piped up.

"A Puritan lady," Eagle replied, recovering his composure. "We're both in the Sealed Knot, but on opposing sides." He smiled.

"And which of these honourable gentleman," Valiant said, tapping the list of attendees, "is the Casanova of the conservatory?"

"His name is Littlejohn, David Littlejohn."

The D.I. could not have been more surprised if he'd said it was Friar Tuck, but he'd work with what they'd got – which wasn't much – for the time being.

"At last," Valiant said triumphantly, "we have a name!"

After learning that the doctor's costume was his own, Valiant asked for the sword so it could be forensically examined. Eagle had to ring his home and ask his wife to bring the sword round to the surgery. He begged the detectives to wait outside for it, which they did, getting wet for their pains.

"Funny, isn't it," Tubby Dale said, as they drove back into Worksop. "A man called Littlejohn, dressing up as Robin Hood."

"Let us hope," said his boss, "that Doctor Eagle has not also been deceived."

A message from the pathologist was waiting for Valiant when he arrived back at Worksop police station. A black thread had been found clinging to the green material of Robin Hood's suit, at the edge of the heart wound. It definitely wasn't hair unless it came from a wig. It hadn't been visible at the time of the post-mortem, with all the clothing being so wet. Under the microscope, traces of blood were observed at one end of the thread.

"I don't know what that proves," said Valiant. "We have neither means, motive nor opportunity so far, but put it on file, Dale."

Dale was on his computer, checking the electoral register for a David Littlejohn.

"Found him, sir. It's a Worksop address right enough. Nobody else registered there, so we should be safe to go in and have a poke around."

Sergeant Scott had returned from her foray into the world of fancy dress.

"You wouldn't believe the range of outfits they've got. Everything from an archbishop's vestments to a body-hugging Lady Godiva suit."

"Yes, well, let's move this investigation on, shall we?" Valiant said. "Angela, you'll come with me. Dale, I want you to check DVLA with Littlejohn's name and address. See if there's a car registered to him. It may well contain his keys and a mobile phone. Either of those would be useful."

Angela Scott was in a talkative mood, as they drove to Littlejohn's house.

"Don't you think it's odd, sir, Littlejohn becoming Robin Hood? Most people would want to be somebody totally different."

"Such as what?"

"I don't know. Buffalo Bill perhaps, or King Arthur or..."

"Or Rin Tin Tin." Valiant finished her sentence. "But what was it that Robin Hood was best known for?"

"Robbing the rich?" she suggested.

"Exactly. But how did our man do it? Sleeping with their wives wouldn't make him rich and we have no reports of thefts at the party, even though they were mostly well off. There was nothing on him when he was found. Unless..."

"Unless what, sir?"

"There is one kind of theft which often doesn't get reported."

"Blackmail, sir?"

"Blackmail, sergeant. But who and why, and why did they kill him rather than pay up?"

They were met at Littlejohn's door by several uniformed officers with a battering ram. After searching around for a key in the usual places, and not finding one, Valiant gave the order to go in.

The small terraced house had, not surprisingly, been fully double-glazed. Inside, they found the rooms unexpectedly tidy. The living room contained a sofa and large screen T.V. Upstairs, along with the bathroom there were two others, one with a double bed and wardrobe, the other empty.

"Where's his computer?" Valiant wanted to know. "Find it, pronto."

"If it's a laptop or an ipad it won't take up a lot of room," Scott observed, returning downstairs and peering under the sofa. She moved on to the kitchen, searching cupboards and the fridge. Finally she turned to the washing machine and opened it up. "Eureka!" she yelled.

She extracted a Compaq laptop, which she placed in an evidence bag. "I'll take this back so we can check all his files and folders. He's a tidy kind of guy. I'm sure, if he is into blackmail, he'll have kept records."

Just then Valiant's phone rang.

"Dale here, sir. We've found Littlejohn's car burnt out in a layby on the A614. Do you still want his keys?"

Littlejohn's laptop hadn't much in the way of security and his files were soon being scrutinised by Sargeant Scott and Tubby Dale. There was a list of people he'd installed double-glazing or conservatories for over the past two years. Doctor Eagle was a name they expected to find, but not Cornelius Ryan.

"He said he didn't know Littlejohn," Dale exclaimed. "He lied to us. A magistrate and he lied!"

"Perhaps he was honestly mistaken," Valiant said. "I don't suppose he'd see much of him while the conservatory was being built. He'd certainly never seen him dressed as a Sherwood outlaw before, or dead for that matter."

"He stayed the night at the hotel next to Clumber Park. He had the opportunity to kill him," Dale protested.

"Opportunity perhaps, but means? Or motive?"

Angela Scott pointed to the screen in front of her. "What do you make of this, Sir?"

She indicated a list of initials with dates next to them, followed by a number, some had 50 or 100 or even 1000 next to them.

"Have we found our blackmail victims, d'you think?" she said.

"We'll need to check his bank account or accounts. See if any sums of the same value were paid in shortly after the dates given here," Valiant said. "If there are, then we can be sure he was blackmailing the people whose initials appear in this list. The trouble is we have only their initials, not their full names. Who, for example, is VE?"

"Valerie Eagle, perhaps," Dale suggested. "I'm sure he called his wife Valerie when he phoned her about the sword."

"Well spotted, Tubby," said Angela Scott. "And I've had another thought. What if the murderer wasn't a man but a woman? There was a geisha costume hired out by the other firm, Party, Party. You know, the Japanese style with dark hair piled on top of the head, held in place by pins that look like knitting needles. If one of them were sharpened, it would make a dandy weapon. And the one from Party, Party in Newark was loaned to Valerie Eagle and returned with one pin missing."

"But Valerie Eagle's a red-head," Dale protested.

"Not if she was wearing a wig," added Valiant. "Bring her in, Angela."

While Sergeant Scott went to Tuxford with a uniformed officer to request Mrs Eagle's presence at the station, Dale was still trying to process the fact that the doctor must have lied to them. If his wife hadn't worn the costume of a Puritan lady but went as a geisha, then he couldn't have driven them both back home after the party. Perhaps he was her accomplice, the one who'd bashed Littlejohn's head in, just to make sure he was dead.

He turned back to checking Littlejohn's bank statements. He'd been very up to date, had this Robin Hood, with internet banking and everything. Yes, the figures were there. They couldn't be denied. He turned back to the list of initials. One who'd paid £2000 to Littlejohn was E.R. "I bet he wasn't sorry Robin Hood was out of the way," thought Dale, "whoever he was."

Valiant was pacing the floor. He hated interviewing women for serious offences, putting pressure on them until they cracked. It went against his nature. He stopped pacing and began raising his heels. It was beginning to annoy Dale.

"Go get yourself a cup of tea and a bun," the D.I. said and sent Tubby scampering off in the direction of the canteen.

"What's this all about? I've done nothing wrong," Valerie Eagle protested as she was led into the interview room, where Inspector Valiant was waiting. Scott sat beside him opposite her. Mrs Eagle looked frightened and worried. If she were innocent, what was she worried and frightened about? At least she hadn't asked for a solicitor. That would just about have nailed it.

Valiant began the questioning. "We know you were being blackmailed by David Littlejohn. Why was that?"

"We had a fling," she began. "My husband was away at a conference and we met, just a couple of times. When I told him it was over, he demanded money not to tell Greg – that's my husband – what we'd been up to. I was shocked when he turned up at the party the other night. But I didn't kill him."

"You hired a geisha costume from" – Valiant consulted his notes – "Party, Party in Newark. You returned it with a pin missing. You said you'd lost it. That wasn't true, was it?"

Mrs Eagle was wringing her hands in obvious agitation. "No," she said.

"You'll have to elaborate on that," Scott said, "otherwise we shall be forced to assume that either you or Doctor Eagle used the missing pin to stab David Littlejohn through the heart. Do you understand what I'm saying?"

"Yes, but that wasn't what happened."

"Was it you who hired the geisha outfit?"

"Yes, but in the end I didn't wear it." She seemed calmer now, as though the crisis was past. "I passed it on to a friend."

"And went to the party as a Puritan Lady instead?" Valiant asked.

"Yes."

"So who was the friend who wore the geisha outfit and 'lost' one of the pins?"

"She wouldn't have killed him. I know she wouldn't."

"Who, Mrs Eagle?"

A full minute's silence followed before she said, in a whisper, "Betty Ryan."

"Louder please, for the tape recording," Valiant said.

"I passed it to Betty Ryan."

Valiant asked if Mrs Ryan were also being blackmailed by Littlejohn, but Mrs Eagle claimed she didn't know. Suddenly it dawned on her that they might both have been in the same predicament. The look of surprise and horror which crossed her face was enough for

Valiant. He said she could go home but must be available if they should want to ask her more questions. She stumbled from the interview room, assisted by a female officer.

Back with Dale and the computer, they told him what Valerie Eagle had told them.

"I knew it wouldn't be her," Dale boasted. "But Betty Ryan? She's not even on his list."

Sergeant Scott, leaning over his shoulder, pointed to the screen. "Yes, she is." Her finger was on E.R. "Betty's an abbreviation for Elizabeth."

"I was afraid this might happen," Valiant said. "We'll have to tread very carefully with this one. Angela, can you get hold of that geisha outfit and wig? I want to check it against the thread that was found on the body." He rubbed his hand across his face. "If it matches, we'll arrest Betty Ryan for murder. She had the means, motive and opportunity."

The Inspector cursed himself for not asking Cornelius Ryan whether his wife had gone to the party in fancy dress. He'd denied doing so himself but had avoided telling them about his wife. Did he know Betty had been involved with David Littlejohn? Did he know she'd killed her lover? Was he even involved with the killing? One thing Valiant knew for sure. He would need to have a cast-iron, double-padlocked, watertight case against one of them or he'd be looking for another job before long.

Betty's demeanour was very different from that of Valerie Eagle, when she was brought to the interview room later that day. Dressed in a smart aquamarine dress and jacket, and flawlessly made up, she was as cool as the proverbial cucumber. In spite of the fact that the black thread matched the wig she'd worn, despite the fact that the police knew she was being blackmailed, and despite Valerie Eagle telling them that she'd supplied Betty with a list of all attendees to the party along with the geisha outfit, she remained unflustered. She'd seen the way all the officers in the station had looked at her and knew she still had the power to attract men, just as she'd attracted Cornelius eighteen years ago. Just as she'd attracted David Littlejohn two years ago.

"It wasn't the money, you know," she told D.I. Valiant, when he'd run through the list of incriminating evidence they had on her. "I had money in my own right before I went to work for Cornelius. I didn't even care if Cornelius knew of the affair. He's an old man and knows he can no longer satisfy my needs, in the bedroom, you understand. He wouldn't have told a soul. What rankled was when I saw David lusting after younger flesh, like Jackie Greenhalgh. I couldn't bear the thought of him telling tales about us, about me, all over the district: what games we used to play and where we used to make love. So I put a stop to it, permanently."

"Are you admitting that you killed David Littlejohn in Clumber Park?"

"Might as well, mightn't I? I knew he was coming to the party, so I sharpened the pin at home beforehand. I arranged to meet him in Clumber for a farewell cuddle."

"Where in Clumber?" Valiant asked.

"The car park in Hardwick," she said. "We walked to the lake as it was a fine night.

It didn't start raining until later. He had the gall to say I was too old for him. So I stabbed him and pushed him into the water. He wasn't dead and tried to climb out again so I picked up a log and hit him with it. Then he slipped back into the lake. I threw both weapons into the water and drove back to the hotel. Cornelius is such a heavy sleeper when he's had a lot to drink, and I made sure he had a lot to drink that night."

"Who moved his car and torched it?" Valiant asked.

" Torched? Where?"

"Further down the A614."

"I didn't know about that. I paid somebody to take it away and lose it." Betty shook her head. "You can't trust anybody these days, can you?"

D.S. Scott escorted her to the cells, and Tubby Dale greeted Valiant as he was coming out of the interview room.

"Satisfactory conclusion, sir?"

"If any murder case can be said to be satisfactory," Valiant replied.

"Cheer up, boss. I'll buy you a pint to celebrate."

"A whole pint?"

"Yes, sir. Nothing's too good for D.I. Intrepid."

"Why you…" But Dale had anticipated his playful punch, and ran off down the corridor, laughing.

JO GALTREY

THE WITCH OF CRESWELL CRAGS

Jo's interest in the natural world and the past began when she first encountered a fossilised trilobite at Doncaster Museum, and was simultaneously given *The Ladybird Book of Dinosaurs*.

Consequently, she was hooked. She went on to work in some amazing museums in London, but has now returned to her roots around Sherwood Forest and is an interpretive guide at Creswell Crags.

THE WITCH OF CRESWELL CRAGS

PROLOGUE

The sound of angry chanting increases as the mob marches nearer. Now the woman is running for her life, through the street and along the river. A snarling splinter group has sheared off and double-backed as she rounds a bend. They spot her and rush in for the kill. There is nowhere else she can go other than down and, clutching her bundle of belongings she takes a great gulp of chilly night air before dropping into the black, bottomless water.

The villagers stare at the rushing river in disbelief, robbed of their quarry. What a motley mix they make: the cheated and diseased, the crippled and the barren, the bitter and bereaved, all clamouring for revenge. And this night revenge has taken the shape of a widowed wife, making ends meet by stitch and by spin, by stitchwort and spindleberry, hemlock and heartsease. Who has goaded this gaggle? None other than the mercurial medic, the fanciful physician who failed to win her hand.

The river runs deep this night but unknown to them, by some miracle or magic, the hag of their collective imagination is coughed up onto the reedy banks of gentler waters, sodden and battered, and still clutching the remnants of her world in a woollen blanket…

From the shadows of the Crags, I watch the visitors read the stone plaque outside the first cave: 'Mother Grundy's Parlour' and I hear them ask, 'Who was Mother Grundy?' The guide replies, as always, 'She was a witch who lived in that cave', but then they are swept onwards, for they have their eye on a far more ancient prize and time is short. But wait! I knew that woman they wonder about. I could tell you more if you would stop and hear my tale. But who am I? I am but one of a throng of spirits who inhabit this land, this corner of the country, this 'neck of the woods' they call The Crags. I was a twig of a lad when she was camping in that cavern. Now we both tread silently with the ancient ones, those who featured here first: the hunters and gatherers, the outlaws and sheriffs, the famous and infamous. No gates can stop us. We whisper and watch the goings-on in the gorge...

To house the hag, you must do this:
Commix with meal a little piss
Of him bewitch'd; then forthwith make
A little wafer or a cake;
And this rawly bak'd will bring
The old hag in. No surer thing.
Robert Herrick 1591 - 1674

Even now, my spirit is drawn towards the river that weaves and wanders through the crags of Creswell as it was then when I was a child and struggling with the challenges of lessons at the chilly village church. The letters, though clear in my head, would become as jumbled on my tongue as they did on the sharp slabs of slate, dished out by the well-meaning Reverend Hogg. This sallow man of the cloth would throw his eyes heavenwards in despair, while at home my flamboyant father, the local physician, raged in disbelief that he could ever have sired 'such a fool' as I.

Whenever I could, I would run as fast as my ten-year old legs would carry me, along the river and into the quiet of the cliffs on the Duke's land; the first duke of this domain though I had never clapped eyes on him. Among its nooks and crannies, I would nestle and gaze at birds flitting about their business or shoals of fish dart and hover in the shallows below. It became my favourite place of escape from school and Bibles and boisterous brothers, though I kept to it by day alone for well I knew the stories of ghosts and witches and wolves recounted nightly by my anxious nurse. But one day I stayed too long: caught up in a reverie, I was caught up in a storm. As fast as I could I slithered from my eyrie and landed on a patch of grass outside a cave, scurrying inside just as the lightning seemed to pierce the cliffs. Shivering and drenched, I crouched transfixed, watching the turmoil outside, though the air around me felt surprisingly still. Still and fragrant. It was only when the storm passed over and the noise receded that I heard the click of a pebble in the rear of that cave, a small pebble being kicked by a foot or a paw. I froze, my spine prickling, my heart thumping in my ears. Someone or something was there, behind me. Then an orange glow began to trace the rocky wall and the shadow of a figure reared up in front of me. I leapt to my feet and backed out of the cave, hurling myself down the bank onto the path, and ran and ran back to the village, vowing never to go near the gorge again.

Mother goose had a house;
It stood in a wood
Where an owl at the door
As a sentinel stood.
Traditional nursery rhyme

After a few more days grappling with scripture and spelling with the rest of the reluctant, I broke my vow and bolted like a rabbit from a trap one sunny morning. Just a few hours of dabbling in the river was all I intended, but it wasn't too long before curiosity got the better of me and I was drawn towards the cave, the cave at the end of the crags.

I tackled the bank at an angle, where I felt sure I was hidden by undergrowth, snaking up as stealthily as I could and peering towards the cave's mouth. It was deserted. After a few more minutes I wriggled out of the brambles and stepped lightly across the rocks, looking left and right, up and down. Nothing. Only the yellow sunshine catching the grass and branches, illuminating the limestone walls. My breath clouded the cool morning air and a flock of sparrows chirped cheekily from some nearby shrubs. I was disappointed more than relieved, cheated of adventure and a little ashamed at my over-active imagination. I slumped down opposite a birch tree near the entrance and plucked at some seed-heads in frustration.

'You need to look more closely, child,' came a sharp voice, a woman's voice. I froze, opened-mouthed, my eyes rolling around trying to see from where the voice came, as if by remaining still I was somehow hidden. 'Why have you returned?'

'I... I... I don't know,' I stammered.

'You can do better than that, young explorer.'

'I... I wanted to know if you were real or if you were...' I trailed off.

'Aha!' came a cackle. 'Real! By that you mean flesh and blood, I take it? Human?'

'Erm, yes.'

'Rather than...what?'

'I don't know.'

'Yes, you do!' The disembodied voice was beginning to sound irritated.

'All right, all right, rather than a monster.'

The voice laughed out loud. 'Then it was a brave move to reappear, my liege. Don't you believe in monsters?'

'Only if I saw one.'

'So, you need evidence! Very scientific. Good answer.'

With that there was a crackling of twigs; then a branch of the birch tree dropped to the ground and walked towards me. Two berry-black eyes were looking down at me from a crinkled brown face, framed by braided grey hair, drawn back close to her head and knotted at the neck with a twist of some kind of plant. A slender hand extended from the grey cloak she wore and shook mine. It was as cool and dry and as papery as the birch but reassuring in its grip.

'Alice Grundy. Pleased to make your acquaintance, young explorer,' she said, looking directly into my face.

At the sight of this apparition (it seemed) I could only stammer, 'I am Tom, Tom the physician's son.'

She paused, then murmured, 'Of course,' with a look of pain in her eyes. Later I was to understand the reason for this pain but then I stared back, oblivious, consumed by the extraordinariness of the day.

'Are you hungry?' she asked me after a moment. Food had been the last thing on my mind, but now it was mentioned I found I was ravenous. 'Lucky I caught TWO fish this morning, then.' She grinned before I had even replied. Two fat trout lay glistening in a shallow rush basket just outside the cave.

'Do you eat them raw?' I asked, peering at the blank stares.

'Sometimes,' she twinkled, 'when I'm in a rush...Eyes and all. Whole. Today, though, I reckon we'll bake them on a fire. What do you think?' I nodded strenuously in relief and also inner amazement, as I was not used to being asked an opinion by my elders, spirits or otherwise. She picked up the basket. 'First, we need wood and herbs. Come on!'

> *Adder's fork and blindworm's sting,*
> *Lizard's leg and owlet's wing,*
> ***William Shakespeare - Macbeth (Act 4, Scene 1)***

After this I would visit Alice Grundy whenever I could, and over that summer I learned more than I ever had before of the world around me, a world teeming with life and mystery – and not a slice of slate nor lump of chalk was ever involved. This magical woman of the woods, as I thought of her, would often appear, as she had at our first meeting, out of nowhere and disappear just as quickly, like a sudden breeze. I would be walking beside her one moment and the next I would find I was talking to a tree or a clump of bulrushes. Then, more often than not, I would hear an urgent voice whisper, 'Thomas, come and see this!' which, if followed, would lead to some treasure of nature: a brightly coloured beetle, a basking lizard or a beautiful moth. I noticed she did this vanishing act if another human appeared on the scene, too, and, like the deer of the forest, she seemed aware of their approach way before I.

To my immense relief there was no more school over the summer, but instead I was often made to accompany my father on his rounds so he could 'keep an eye on me' and show me 'some sense'. Most of the time the visits he paid were in the village: Widow Fletcher's youngest with a rash, the Smithy's twins with colic or the return of old Mother Turner's gout. I was instructed to sit quietly and not to 'make a nuisance of myself', and I tried hard for I knew if behaved the more time I would be awarded to go on my own adventures. My father approached his patients in the same manner he reserved for children, including myself. His voice boomed from behind his beard and he would throw his great frame among their fragile furniture, delighting in impressing his patients with his immense store of knowledge. He talked much of 'humours', especially phlegm and bile, and one his favourite remedies were 'powders' that boasted the inclusion of unicorn horn and other such wonders, though I was sure I had only ever seen him grinding up garden snails and chalk. The most dramatic of remedies was the bleeding of the patient using large and loathsome leeches that he kept in a crock of foetid water and starved for this very purpose.

The absence of school meant more time to visit the Crags but my lessons continued without me being aware. 'What is this?' Alice asked me one day, pointing to a large, long-leaved plant growing by the river. I had no idea and confessed as much. 'What about this one?' she continued, drawing the crook of her hazel staff around another tall plant.

'Nettle,' I replied with confidence.

'Mmmph' she snorted. 'We have much work to do, young explorer.' From then she would have me study meticulously the many varieties of plant and tree that lived along the gorge: their appearance and smell, their texture and sometimes taste, where they grew and how they thrived. Later, the lessons leaned towards their incorporation in salves and poultices, cordials, teas and tinctures. I was amazed at the breadth of their uses and never tired of learning more. Eventually I was able to witness their real effects, for occasionally I would accompany Alice to some far-flung farm or isolated dwelling place where help was needed, and in exchange for food or materials she passed these powerful potions into grateful hands.

'How do you cure someone of poison?' I asked one day.

'With poison,' she said simply, 'but you have to know which poison to pick.' I was unusually quiet as I pondered this reply and asked nothing more that day.

It appeared that not everyone was convinced about my father's apothecary, especially Giles Goodwin, the old shepherd. 'He can keep them ol' leeches to 'imself,' he wheezed one day when my father had briefly left the bedroom of the hut that Giles and his wife Margaret called home.

‘Why?’ I asked, intrigued

‘If your mother was still around, God rest her soul, then she’d be telling you… last thing she needed were those great gobbets of goo sucking the life out of ‘er… .’ He broke off as my father returned. I was fascinated and wanted to ask him more, for people rarely spoke to me of my mother, who had died when I was born; but alas, Giles clammed up once more and my father took over with swaggering joviality and pushed a packet of powders into the shepherd’s thin hands before taking his leave, with me in tow. I noticed Giles merely coughed wearily and let the packet fall onto the counterpane with a defeated sigh, and I felt sad for my old friend.

> *Goe burne these poys’nous weedes in yon blew fire,*
> *These Screech-owles fethers, and this prickling bryer,*
> ***Thomas Campion 1567 - 1620 – A Lute Song***

When I got the chance, I told Alice about the ailing Giles and quizzed her about the merits of leeches and powders as she stewed some purplish plant stems in a small iron pot over the fire. It smelt odious, like the back of the outhouses, where the mice scampered. She replied to my question darkly, ‘Why draw the blood of one with none to spare?’

‘How do you mean?’ I asked as I poked about in some of the plants she had by the fire.

‘Don’t touch those!’ she snapped suddenly. I jumped back, stung. ‘I am sorry to alarm you, Thomas,’ she continued more gently, ‘but they are very poisonous. You should know that by now.’

‘I’m sorry,’ I said quickly, desperate to get back to my mission of making the old shepherd better. ‘Can you help Giles?’

‘Giles is very old and very poorly, Thomas,’ she said with a frown as she poured some of the brew into a clay phial and stoppered it with a plug of soft wax, ‘but I can make something up to ease him.

I'll take it to Margaret when night falls.'

'Thanks, Alice!' I beamed as I clambered down from the cave. It was only when I was halfway home did I realise I had never spoken of Giles's wife before nor mentioned where they lived – so how did Alice know?

That evening, Hannah, the miller's niece called on my father and begged him to attend her uncle, who had taken ill on his return from making a delivery up-stream to one of the farms. With no one else to mind us at that hour, my father marched me and my small step-brothers to the mill and instructed us to wait in the large kitchen, but before long we were peering around the door curiously. The miller was as pale as his flour and gripped my father's arm as a drowning man would. 'I saw her, doctor,' he whispered hoarsely. 'I saw her up near the woods, walking this way… water and weed clinging to her hair and neck, her arms out-stretched.' At this, my father's florid cheeks also mysteriously drained of colour, too. Hannah was hovering in the doorway and I hissed, 'Who does he mean?' She turned to me and whispered dramatically, 'The witch they turned out when you were but a babe, the one who drowned in the river… she's back!'

'A witch!' My little brothers' eyes widened in awe and excitement.

'Aye,' continued Hannah, 'a witch with a mark on her wrist, like a splash of ink… the mark of the devil,' she added with a flourish and left the room.

In the following few days it was my chief occupation to sit with certain patients and read to them or make small talk while my father attended to other matters, and in this manner I heard mention of 'the witch' in many a creaking cottage, for like a sudden flurry of autumn leaves, the story was everywhere. Some goggled at this ghoulish tale, while others dismissed such 'tittle-tattle', but more than a handful became mysteriously mute and I noticed my father was one such person.

At home, too, the appearance of the ghost was the source of much below-stairs banter. 'If you ask me,' said Mary, our cook, slapping a great hunk of dough about on the scrubbed oak trestle with plump hands 'all she did was try and help the poor souls as can't afford bloomin' unicorn powder and the likes. She's been sorely missed these past years.' She puffed out her cheeks and slapped the bread mix down again while I nibbled a jam tart under the table. ''E loved her once, your father, but her 'art went with her 'usband to 'is grave.'

'That's enough, Mary,' snapped Mrs Mason, the housekeeper, 'and you,' she said, jabbing a bony finger at me, 'out!' I emerged from my corner and scarpered before sharp-tongued Mrs Mason could say any more.

> *Away, away, you ugly witch*
> *Hold far away and let me be*
> ***Alison Gross - Traditional Ballad***

Early the next morning there was a loud banging at the door; then an urgent voice shouted, 'Can you come quick, Doc?' Further muffled conversation followed then I heard someone say ''E took a draught and now e's dead.' I couldn't hear the rest, and my first thought was that it must be the poor terror-struck miller, but to my horror I found it was Giles who had died in the night. Fear filled my mind. What medicine had Alice given him? And who was Alice Grundy? An outsider that no one here knew about except me? A terrible thought bubbled in my brain... Could Alice be the witch Hannah told me about last night? If she was, then it was her ghost I had been seeing... My father grabbed his bag and was hurrying out the door as he shouted, 'Stay where you are Thomas,' but even as the door shut behind him I knew I needed to see Alice Grundy, and, come flesh or phantom, I needed to know what potion she had brewed for old Giles.

I almost ran into her as I sprinted along the gorge path, as if she knew I would appear. She grabbed my shoulders, bringing me to a standstill like a runaway pony and looked into my now tear-stained face with her bird-like eyes. 'What has happened, Thomas?' she asked, leading me up to the cave as I spluttered and sobbed out the story. She listened with a frown, lifting her head up sharply when I mentioned the miller's encounter with the ghost of a witch.

'What was in it?' I asked, and even as I said this I knew in a flash that some of the plants she'd had by the fire the previous day must have been in the sleeping draught. I looked down at her hands and for the first time I spotted the blotch of darkened skin, 'like a splash of ink' Hannah had said, and THERE it was.

'It IS you!' I shouted, standing up abruptly. 'You ARE that witch!'

'Thomas.'

'You're a witch and you poisoned him!'

'Thomas. No!'

'You knew his wife's name without me telling you and you cursed the village, everyone says so!' Even as I'd spoken I could hear the empty childishness of my words, but could not find a way to stop myself.

"Everyone', Tom? Who do you mean by 'everyone'?'

But I refused to listen and jumped onto the path below and ran away as fast as I could, but I soon slowed down to a dejected walk.

When I finally arrived home, my mind had been turning over and over the events of the past few hours. My whole world had collapsed. I had destroyed my friendship with Alice in a few sentences and I had yet to confront my father, who must know by now that I had been scheming with a witch! Worse still, I had to face Giles's wife, Margaret. I entered the house via the back door and through the kitchen. Thankfully no one was about as I plodded reluctantly up the back stairs. As I approached the parlour I heard low voices, and I prepared to slip silently past when the door opened and my father stood over me, his face grey and implacable. 'Where have you been?' he asked in a flat tone that unnerved me far more than his usual shouting. 'I told you to stay at home'.

'I... I went to see someone... someone I know,' I mumbled. Then I looked up and beside him was Margaret Goodwin. I could feel my face drain of colour and hung my head low, expecting the worst. 'We will discuss that later, Thomas, but now right now I have other matters to attend to,' and with that he leapt up the stairs two at a time and I was left with Margaret, the old shepherd's wife.

'I'm sorry about Giles,' I murmured. 'It was that potion she gave you, wasn't it?'

Margaret was silent for a moment, then crouched beside me and said firmly, 'No, Tom. It was his time. The potion, as you call it, eased his pain.'

I couldn't believe my ears. 'Really?' I asked, looking up into her face. 'But I thought... I thought...'

'You thought it was poison?'

'Yes,' I whispered, then added, 'Do you know Alice Grundy?'

She looked momentarily surprised. 'Alice? Yes, I do, though I know her by a different name. She's my oldest friend... and she was a very good friend of your mother's, too.'

'Oh!' I exclaimed, agog at this revelation. 'But is she a witch?'

'No, Tom! She's a very kind and wise woman with her ear and eye to the mysteries of nature, and she knows how to harness its powers, but unfortunately, when folks don't get the answer they want, they turn around and call it witchcraft.'

Now I was silent. Then a new realisation dawned on me and I asked her hesitantly, 'Does that include my father?'

'Unfortunately, Tom, yes, it does.'

'Is that why he is angry about the… the medicine Alice gave Giles?'

'Your father doesn't know anything about that, Thomas, and as far as he's aware, Alice, as you call her drowned in the river when she was chased out of the village when you were a baby… He isn't angry, he's troubled.'

'About the ghost?' I asked with youthful simplicity.

'About the ghost, yes, but perhaps more because he realises he was wrong to accuse her.'

I thought about this a few moments, then said with sudden anguish, 'I need to see Alice! I was horrible to her, too!'

'At least you can make amends, Tom, though I fear it might be too late for your father, God forgive him.'

By magic or miracle or, most probably, the inescapable pattern of nature, an opportunity for reconciliation arose far more swiftly than either of us could anticipate, for that very evening my lively little brothers fell ill after playing in the garden. 'We were making a lovely blue potion,' was all William could whisper to our father as he fell into a pallid sleep, and when Mary and I hunted around we found a little pot of petals by the back door: Monkshood petals. Mary broke down and sobbed when she spied this innocent but deadly concoction, crying, 'There's nothing to be done! The poor bairns, they're doomed!' My father, the physician, slumped into a chair, his great head in his hands, knowing that none of his marvellous medicines, powders or leeches would remedy this ruin.

But I knew what to do. I knew the one person who could help and sprang from my seat and was gone, racing along the river towards the Crags.

> *A witche, and not a witche, and yet a witche indeede.*
> ***Nicholas Breton (16th Century)***

My youthful head had no idea what I was asking of her when I implored her to help my brothers that day, but with me she came, pale of face, tender of heart and brave of spirit, to face the foe once more. The villagers peered from their houses with fearful faces, no doubt sure this phantom had come to claim a justified revenge on them, but all Alice Grundy carried was a concoction, an intricate infusion of foxglove, which she administered to the afflicted infants: a poison for a poison, while a noose of silence stretched around that room and the minutes ticked by…

Tick-tock, tick-tock, tick-tock.

Then, little by little, my brothers breathed again.

Those who had damned were discredited that day and, shame-faced, they begged her to return to them for good, but all she replied as she walked away was, 'I am content in my cave. I have found my niche. Now leave me in peace.' I felt empty at this ending, but then she stopped and turned and pointed straight at me, saying 'Except YOU. You may come and pester me as often as you please. There is still much to learn.'

And so, I did, and eventually I, too, became a doctor, much to the surprise of my father and the Reverend Hogg – and what is more, I never used a single leech.

There is a cave at Creswell Crags called Mother Grundy's Parlour and legend has it that she was a woman who was banished from the village (presumably Creswell) for being a witch and came and lived In that cave. One day she saved the life of a child, and she was pardoned and invited to return to the village, but she chose to live in the cave for the rest of her life. In an alternative version, she saved the life of the Duke of Portland's son; however, having checked with the curatorial team at the Welbeck estate, there is no record in the, apparently, well-documented lives of the Dukes of any event involving the character Mother Grundy or anyone fitting her description. I therefore set this story during a period in Britain when superstitions ran high and witch-hunts were rife, but who Mother Grundy really was or when she lived, if she ever existed at all, may remain a mystery.

SUSAN AMELIA MOSS

YOUR GRACE

I grew up in a small Hamlet in South Wales. There were no shops, just one church, a rectory, five farms, and a few houses. It stood proudly on three levels, looking out over the moors and the River Thaw, providing the children with many adventures.

It was memories of these adventures that created the writer in me. As a child, I loved reading (and still do), from Shakespeare to modern crime thrillers and, most recently, *The Pilgrim's Progress* by John Bunyan.

Over the years I have put pen to paper, and now spend hours at the computer writing the stories I made up to entertain my children and grandchildren.

I'm currently working on my second novel; at sixty-nine years of age it keeps my mind active. I've even been known to create an adventure story, with full character names, whilst walking with friends through the woods.

It was while walking the grounds of Clumber Park that I felt the need to explore further into the limited information given on the Lincoln, a wreck of a small frigate, that, during a very dry period is said to be visible.

It was then that I created a character that would take the reader not only on an historical journey, but a character with imagination, a sense of humour and compassion.

YOUR GRACE

Monday 27th March in the year 2010, a year that was to change my life forever. I have documented what took place on that day, as a true and honest account and stored it safely on disc for whosoever is interested in delving into my remarkable experience. Maybe I should say experiences, as over the years I have encountered many more fascinating adventures, that were just as, or possibly more exciting, but for now, I shall concentrate only on the events of that day.

It was on that particular day that I had found myself, for no reason other than having had a few cross words with my wife, rather melancholy as I began my journey. I proceeded with the usual weekly drive to North Nottinghamshire Clumber Park, only this time without my wife, as on this occasion she refused to accompany me. We had enjoyed many walks each time we ambled towards our favourite resting place at Clumber Bridge. But on that day, especially because I was on my own, I had felt compelled to reach the bridge as quickly as I could.

Perhaps somewhere in my subconscious, especially after reading about its history, I felt drawn to take in the true exquisiteness of my surroundings. Until that day, the bridge always happened to be just our first resting place, where we'd discuss our plans for the rest of the day. But the compulsion to see and study Clumber Bridge, since I had gained a little knowledge of a possible family connection, had begun a fire in my body that I hadn't felt before.

Before reaching the bridge, and at varying intervals, I felt a compulsion to stand and survey what I thought the Dukes of Newcastle-under-Lyne would have probably taken for granted. It had only been two weeks earlier, upon reading about the four ducal seats – Welbeck

Abbey, Thoresby Hall, Worksop Manor and Clumber House – that my interest became more of an obsession. These places I had visited many times, but the one that interested me most was, Clumber House and the Dukes of Newcastle, and, of course, their name.
After discovering that we, my wife and I, had the same names as the 4th Duke and his wife (I'm Henry Pelham and my wife is Georgiana), I had become possessed with finding out as much about them as I could, with the notion that there could possibly be a connection to my family. Although we don't have as many children, I believe they had eleven surviving heirs. We had named our sons Thomas and Charles, as did the 4th Duke and his wife, Georgiana. 'It's just coincidental,' my wife had said, as I gathered as much information as I could muster off the internet; she was also adamant that the child she was expecting would be the third and last of the children that we had planned.

Not satisfied with the internet and library, I dabbled in a form of self-hypnosis. It allowed me to focus on my inner self, bring out hidden memories and heighten my response to suggestion. I became fixated with finding out as much as I could, as I now firmly believed that I was a definite descendant of the 4th Duke of Newcastle. It was driving my poor wife to distraction.

Although I had, each and every time that I had walked the trail at Clumber Park, enjoyed every aspect of its magnificent serpentine lake, woodland and array of wildlife, my goal this time was to approach it as never before. My stride was purposeful as I made my way in the direction of the bridge.

Spring could definitely be felt in the air; it was a welcome reminder that winter had, once and for all, been left behind. I could smell the fragrance of the blossom as I passed beneath the trees. A young woman sat on one of the rustic benches beside the lake; her nails were digging deep into an orange, causing the peel to release a powerful aroma. I could smell the zest of the orange as its juices burst into the air; a gentle breeze just at the right time showered me with its spray.
I nodded in acknowledgement as I glanced in her direction. She smiled, then hurriedly opened the fruit for a child of about three or

four years of age. He hovered beside her. It was obvious that the fruit was well received, but his anxiety to get to the lake took preference as he swiftly took the segment of orange, stuffed it quickly into his mouth and dashed without her towards the edge of the water. He had a small paper bag in his hand; it bulged with whatever was treasured inside. Food for the ducks and swans, I thought, as I felt a relief that she had caught up with him. I smiled to myself and continued on my way.

The air felt fresh as I filled my lungs with the deepest breath that I had taken that morning. I purposefully took myself off the trail to follow a narrow, winding track beside the lake. I'd noticed it on my last walk and had tried to persuade my wife to follow it with me, but she hadn't wanted to walk so close to the lake. Dew from the budding leaves dropped onto my face as my hair caught on one of the low boughs. Just for a moment it gave me a strange but pleasant feeling, as though something magical was about to happen. I untangled myself, then ducked below the boughs to emerge into a small clearing. It gave me a sense of adventure as I excitedly hopped across the small gully that had been created by erosion, possibly from animals approaching their drinking place at the edge of the lake.

As I steadied myself after slipping dangerously close to the edge I looked up; the bridge had suddenly come into view. It must have been about fifty metres away. It startled me slightly as I hadn't expected to reach it so quickly, but there it was in all its full glory. I felt a compulsion to close my eyes and savour what I had missed before. I must have stood with my eyes closed for almost two mins. Again, I took in a deep breath before slowly opening my eyes, expecting to see with clarity the architecture that I had at other times taken for granted. I wasn't disappointed.
The bridge looked magnificent. I had never before seen it in the manner that I saw it that day. Obviously my dabbling in hypnosis had opened my mind to the beauty of my surroundings. The vista before me appeared to create a freedom of anticipation.

My body suddenly shuddered as a strange feeling enveloped me.

It drew my attention away from the bridge towards the lake. I felt compelled to glance across the lake to where I knew that the Dukes' magnificent house had stood in its day. Trees and shrubbery towered where the building once was. I stared as though in a hypnotic state, willing myself back to the time of the 4th Duke of Newcastle-under-Lyne. That was when I believed, at the time, that my imagination had begun to run away with me. I saw fountains, benches and ornamental statues, standing proudly around a beautiful landscaped garden. Stone urns either side of stone seats furthered my imagination as I brought to life what each Duke had added to transform the gardens. I added drama by including the model of a gun battery threateningly pointing out towards the lake. It was a most exhilarating sight.

I embraced my imagination until it was disturbed by a sound, a whisper, a whisper that made me turn around to see who was standing so close. But there was no-one; I was alone; only the whisper still lingered in the air. There was no rustling from the trees that surrounded me, there were no squirrels scurrying about, not even a breeze of such that could carry a sound, but the whisper was still there.

An eeriness crept about me as a mist began rising from the lake. I could no longer see trees or shrubs or even the picture of the magnificent house that I desperately tried to bring back into my imagination. The dense mist moved its way slowly but surely in my direction. It hovered for a moment in front of me, as if deciding whether to encase me with a shroud of its eeriness, before passing slowly by. As it moved on, it left a trail of emptiness, not unpleasant, but different; the scenery was different. Where tall trees and shrubs had dominated the view at the other side of the lake, and I had to use my imagination to create the scene that I required. Now, in its place, landscaped gardens and buildings were once again visible. It was as though I had actually been transported back in time. I was in awe of the vista before me and no longer had to use my imagination. My attention was drawn once again to the mist as it crept slowly towards the bridge. It hovered again as if checking to see that I was still watching, before rising purposefully, encapsulating the three arches then weaving its way between the balustrades that adorned

the top. There was a moment of disbelief and I began to blink rapidly as though trying to awaken from a dream. I pinched myself just to make sure that I wasn't dreaming, then watched as the mist hung like the theatre drapes of a stage curtain, as if it was about to reveal the First Act.
I became fascinated by the form that had appeared before me. I stared in wonderment as I stood at the side of the lake, my eyes now transfixed on nothing other than the curtain of mist that was slowly beginning to fade. The limestone of the bridge glistened from the refraction of light as the mist traced its way along each curve.

For years it had just been the bridge, a resting place and a means of getting my wife and me back to the car after enjoying an early morning stroll around the lake. But today, because of my determination to connect myself to its history, it fascinated me. The grandeur of the Palladian style reached into the depths of a memory, perhaps a memory that had been passed on from another generation, or maybe the recent memory of what I had read; I opted for the former. I had also been dabbling with regression lately but had been afraid to take it too far.

Perhaps it was the melancholy shroud that had followed me that morning, the angry words that I had had with my wife before leaving. My constant obsession with Clumber Park, Sherwood and the Dukeries –I knew it had begun to put a strain on our marriage. I also began to question my sanity. Had this recent knowledge started to play with my mind? Why did I feel the urgency to find a connection? What if my dabbling with the unknown had caused a depression in me that was now out of control? But the melancholy that I had felt that morning had lifted the moment that I had driven through the magnificent gate into the park. It was as if I had seen, for the first time, its grandeur.

Of course, I had admired the architecture of the gate each and every time that I had visited before, but not felt its splendour and impressiveness of appearance and style as I had that day.

As the mist began to clear, I noticed a group of people standing on the bridge; they were excitedly pointing towards the lake. But there was definitely something different about them. For a moment I couldn't fathom it out, until I realised that they were either in fancy dress or I'd stepped back in time; again I began to question myself. Had I really been mysteriously transported back in time? Or was the scene that had begun to play out in front of me a re-enactment, a theatre group warming up for their performance later in the day? It wasn't unusual for Clumber Park to stage entertainment and, of course, the theatre group would have to rehearse at some time. I blinked a few times to clear my head, but they were still there. I felt disbelief and a thrill of unexpectedness as a pleasant chill once again began to envelope my entire body. I now felt compelled to walk towards the bridge.

For a moment, I hoped to see other spectators, as I had convinced myself that I had come across a theatre group. I glanced quickly around me; I saw the old woman in her faded purple raincoat, which, whether it was much too hot for a coat, or whether it was wet, cold and windy, she wore loosely about her person as she walked her small terrier dog. She always looked troubled, but then she'd smile; her eyes were kind as they'd show recognition as I walked by. I'd nodded and spoken many times before. Then there was the young woman in a white track suit who looked as though she had just stepped out of a magazine; her hair and makeup was immaculate as she tried to keep up with a young man in dark shorts and a t-shirt. There was something written across the front of his shirt, but I could never fathom out what it said. He always looked as though he was trying to impress her as he flexed his muscles with each stride. They would smile and say hello, as did many others, either as groups as they strolled past often in deep conversation, or cyclists heading in another direction; someone always took the time to speak. But not today. I appeared to be the only spectator of the event that I felt was to be played out in front of me. I ventured nearer.

"Come along," called a figure as it beckoned me to join the crowd that was still gathering on the bridge (there must have been about twenty). "We have the best view," he said as he hurried over to me and took hold of my hand. He shook it firmly but seemed distracted by something. I followed his gaze across the lake. "It's your 'Lincoln,'" he said. "Isn't it splendid?"

I'd read of the 'Lincoln' and the 'Salamanca' both being used as a summerhouse for the 4th Duke of Newcastle, and thought that it was wonderful that someone had managed to float a replica. I turned my body and stood proudly facing the lake. "Splendid!" I said as I watched the impressive vision unfold before me. Three masts stood proudly as if waiting for the order to raise the sails. I closed my eyes momentarily to savour the moment.

"Father." A child's voice was heard beside me. Then a small hand pushed into mine. "I can't see!" the young child urged. It pulled at my sleeve with as much urgency and excitement in his voice as I had begun to feel in myself. I allowed myself to venture nearer to the balustrade, then glanced down at the child.

Somehow, I knew what my part was to be. My heart raced with trepidation, unsure that I was good enough for the part that had just been thrust upon me. A deep breath from me and the nod of encouragement from the group that was awaiting my next move reassured me that it was much more than a walk-on bit-part.

"The child – he's yours," called a voice from the crowd.

"Mine!" I mouthed in surprise. "Of course he is!" I answered. I glanced down at the bubbly child; my heart melted at the sight of his cherub-like face, but my head found difficulty in recognising him.

"Lift him up!" another voice called as it came nearer.

Searching from where the voice came, I saw another child, a young girl not much older than the young boy beside me. I glanced vaguely at them both, unsure of how to handle the situation when another voice of a much older child called their names. "Henry, Georgiana, leave Father alone. You have been requested to meet Grandfather on the terrace," the child said, with urgency in her voice.

Ah yes, the terrace, I thought as I swiftly glanced around me; I'm needed for the launch. I couldn't believe that I had the chance,

although I knew it could only be a replica, that I had the privilege of being in the right place at the right time and had been chosen to take the lead.
"I do apologise, Your Grace," called a young woman as she hurried towards us with yet another, younger, child holding tightly on to her skirt, attempting to keep pace. "They saw you from the garden. It's the excitement of the launch," she added as she hastily took charge of the young boy.

The laughter and chatter from the children lifted what had been a moment of pensiveness to one of elation. "They are mine; they are all mine," I whispered to myself as I walked briskly in the same direction. I felt the need to skip occasionally, but decided it inappropriate if I was to be the 4th Duke of Newcastle. I surveyed with pride the crowd of people that had gathered to watch the launch of the 'Lincoln'.

"Well done, old chap," an aged voice whispered in my ear. I turned to see an elderly-looking, extremely distinguished, gentleman, and immediately fell into the character of Henry Pelham Fiennes Pelham-Clinton, 4th Duke of Newcastle-under-Lyne.

"Edward!" I exclaimed. I had no trouble in recognising my wife's father as I smiled with pride and pointed to the sails of the frigate. "Do you think she'll like it?" I asked, as I nodded to the young sailor who was to take charge of the vessels. I say 'vessels' as the 'Salamanca' could now be seen beside the 'Lincoln'.

"I love it!" a sweet comforting voice whispered beside me. I turned to see Georgiana smiling at me. Her hands were placed lovingly across the rather large bump of her stomach.

"You shouldn't be out here in your condition," I replied and swiftly swept her into my arms. She protested in the most charming manner any man could desire as I carried her into the house. "I promise, in the next few years I'll commission someone to set out borders and fountains," I said, as I placed her gently onto one of the window seats.

"We'll call it the 'Lincoln Terrace'," she said as she winced with pain.

"Ah yes, the Lincoln Terrace – that's exactly what it will be called." I repeated this to myself as I hesitantly moved away from her.

"If it's a boy, we shall call him John or perhaps Lincoln," she teasingly announced as she waved me out of the house. "It's your day, Henry. Enjoy it!" she called as I walked with as much decorum as I possibly could towards the waiting crowd.

"Your Grace," I thought I heard someone say as I looked out over the lake. I was enjoying every minute of being transported back to 1817. I knew it to be that particular year as I recalled reading about it only a week before. So I joined in with such enthusiasm that I had now begun to believe that I actually was Henry Pelham, 4th Duke of Newcastle-under-Lyne. It gave me an air of superiority over the crowds that were gathering to watch the launch, and I liked it. I nodded in acceptance at the few who called to me, even thinking that I recognised one or two. I was lost in what my mind believed to be a re-enactment but my heart longed for to be real. I glanced out at the one-third scale naval frigate with pride and watched the magnificent sails being hoisted.

"It's time, Your Grace," a voice whispered beside me. I took this to be my cue to approve the launching of the 'Lincoln', and strode purposefully towards the crowd that had now created enough room for me to walk in a regal manner towards the awaiting dais. The applause was thunderous as I walked forward.
I stepped on the dais and looked out over the crowds toward the house; to my surprise, there was nothing there. Perhaps the scenery had been moved, I thought, as my brain struggled with the concept of imagination and reality. The house – it had felt so real. And Georgiana – I'd left her in so much pain; it made me think of the heartache that I had left my wife in that morning. I dismissed any thoughts of the present time as quickly as they came: I didn't want to lose the atmosphere of the moment.

It was then that I felt a disappointment that tore at my heart. It was a sinking feeling that couldn't be described. I felt compelled to turn and face the lake. As I turned, I felt a warmth brush across the cheeks of my face. I instantly put my hands up to protect my eyes, but through the gaps of my fingers I could see flames.

To my horror, the 'Lincoln' was on fire. I gasped at the inferno that had now taken the place of the launch. How cruel, I thought, to take me on such a wonderful experience, only to destroy the memory so quickly. "There's nothing for you here," someone whispered beside me. "We've moved on one hundred and twenty-two years."

I was about to ask whoever it was who was standing beside me, why such a leap in time? But the same mist that had moved across the lake earlier had returned. It enveloped the burning 'Lincoln'. When I eventually tore myself away from the fading vision of the burning wreck and glanced around me, there was no-one; once again I was on my own.

Although I knew that I had seen the 'Lincoln' burning, and that I had been part of what I still believed to be a re-enactment, I was beginning to doubt my sanity. Why had everyone disappeared? Was it part of the show? Would they, all of a sudden, reappear and continue with my inclusion in the drama? I stared towards the mist, expecting to see as I did at the bridge, the image of a theatre curtain, only this time for it to rise to reveal an audience. The applause would be deafening. I would take the first bow. But there was no-one and nothing, only the skeletal remains of a wreck slowly sinking beneath the water. As the waters became once again still, I stared in disbelief at my surroundings.

The lake was calm: no breeze not even a ripple; the only movement came from the swans, mallards and moorhens bobbing about on the surface. I found myself once again following the track beside the lake and meandering my way towards the bridge. It was as if my experience had never happened. As I stooped below the low branches, I heard a whisper in the breeze that had suddenly appeared from nowhere. I looked up and caught the glimmer of sunshine as it sparkled off the limestone of the three arches of the bridge; a mist had gathered below. It rose slowly, weaving itself through the balustrades just as it had before. I held my breath in anticipation of déjà vu.

A hand rested on my shoulder as if trying to comfort me. It startled me for a moment before I realised it was the old lady in her faded purple raincoat. It hung loosely about her person. Her sad eyes looked deep into mine; she looked anxious as she asked me if I was all right, before asking me if I had seen her dog. "He's a small white terrier," she said as she hurried away. "Perhaps he's crossed the bridge."

"Would you like me to help you?" I asked as I ran to catch up with her as she sprinted swiftly toward the bridge.

There was a group of people standing on the bridge; one in particular was pointing towards something far out into the lake. I held my breath in anticipation of his next words. "Come along! We have the best view!" the young man called as he encouraged the others to look.

I held my breath as I glanced out across the lake: part of me wanted to experience the events that I believed had happened to me only moments ago, and part of me unsure that they had taken place at all. My eyes swiftly scanned the lake. Three magnificent sails were proudly rising as I brought the 'Lincoln' into my mind. I watched in amazement as it sailed gracefully towards me. "Your Grace!" I thought I heard someone say.

A hand touched my shoulder; it was the same young man who had beckoned to me earlier. "Aren't they graceful!" he said, his voice full of excitement. It's the first time that I have seen them in flight."

The vision of the 'Lincoln' morphed into three beautiful swans as they flew effortlessly towards us. Once again, my mind had played tricks with me, or had I somehow, just for a second or so, managed to step back in time? The young man, I noticed, had continued on

his way, his experience still being played out to his friends as he flailed his arms above his head, displaying the magnificence of the flight of the three swans.
Suddenly, a small hand grasped mine and pulled me back to the edge of the lake. It was the same child who had been anxious to feed the ducks earlier; his mother paced apprehensively besides the water's edge. She beckoned us to quickly come to her. "Edward, quickly bring the gentleman to me," she called. "I'm afraid the little dog has upset the swans: they have him cornered." There certainly was a commotion about two metres out onto the lake, but, as far as I could see, the little dog had the situation well in hand – or is that in paw? He looked slightly bedraggled as he paddled his way effortlessly towards his distressed mistress.
The old lady in the faded purple coat began to sink to her knees. For a second or two I was torn between cajoling the little dog out of the water and comforting the old lady. My instincts told me that the dog could take care of itself, so I swept her into my arms and carried her swiftly to the park bench. I had the strangest feeling of once again being the 4th Duke of Newcastle-under-Lyne, and an overwhelming need to protect Georgiana, my wife – or was it to protect the unborn child that she was carrying? I fought against the urgency of being with my wife as I once again saw the stressed look of the old lady, and placed her gently beside the young woman and child before turning to face the lake. The sopping wet dog shook himself to dry off before running past me to the arms of his mistress; the child and his mother fussed over them both.

I wandered to the bridge once again and leaned my body against the balustrade. My back was towards the lake, my mind now on my wife whom I had left at home; how distressed she must have been after the cross words that I had said to her only an hour or two before. The temptation to look back over the lake and to wander through the trees and bushes to where the old house once stood and perhaps, once again, experience what it was like to be the 4th Duke had been overruled by the overwhelming guilt of leaving my wife at home, especially in her condition.

That day I left the park with the feeling of accomplishment: whether

I was a descendant of the 4th Duke or just a twenty-first century countryman with the expectation of a 'facade of grandeur', it really had no relevance.

Knowledge, combined with self-hypnosis, can create a wonderful phenomenon. I had only just, that day, touched on the edge of adventure, although I must admit it took me quite a few attempts for my brain to accept that I had travelled in time. I questioned myself many times before accepting the gift that many would love to possess. I have visited many times and will continue to experience life in the past, and one day I'll take my daughter Georgiana on a journey to meet her distant relations, as, at seven years of age, she has already begun to show an interest.

MEL E GOLD

THE MAGICKER OAK

Mel E Gold is an American citizen who moved to the Land of Tea and Irony thirteen years ago after marrying her British husband.

In addition to writing, Mel spends her free time singing in a local heavy metal band called *Aonia* and is a guest backing vocalist on the latest two albums by Blaze Bayley (ex-Iron Maiden).

This is Mel's second contribution to the North Nottinghamshire Short Story Competition – her short story "Promised Land" was featured in the 2016 edition of the compilation.

By day, Mel is secondary school English teacher. She began writing fiction while teaching an A-level Creative Writing course, and fell in love with creating what her editor calls "word pictures".

Mel would like to thank her husband, her family, her writing buddies Graham and Harry, and her editor, Gabby, for their support.

THE MAGICKER OAK

The sorcerer sliced through the moonlight, dancing the dance of the damned. Pulling fire from the sky, he held it for a fleeting eternity in his hands and released it toward his dark enemies.

Skeletons, imbued with life, jolted forward in droves through the choking trees. Graves opened, and their sleepers waked, grey skins sallow in the moonlight, shuffling forward before the flames drove them back.

Goblins, ghouls, ghosts, shadows, spirits, and demons – all suffocated the figure, a raw-boned man in his early twenties with long, dark hair and a thick beard. He held a small dagger as a weapon and no shield, protected only by a long, evergreen robe (emblazoned with the image of an oak tree cradling the sun in its leaves) and a translucent sphere that shimmered and shimmied and threatened to collapse.

The spellcaster's voice rattled through Sherwood Forest. "Help! The charm's collapsing!"

A glint of a silver short-sword. A brown pointed cowl concealing an amber cascade of hair. A fighter.

Slight of stature and narrow-shouldered, the fighter swung the short-sword at the otherworldly assailants, each vanishing in a puff of sulphurous smoke the moment the rapier's tip touched their formless bodies.

As he re-cast the wards, Silvaro whispered, "Did you change your weapon?"

"Holy water," came the grunted reply.

"It works."

"Stop talking and throw some fireballs at them."

Flames scorched across the sky.

One dark creature, two more, three more, six more, and then another six descended toward the pair. The short-sword destroyed all it touched – but it could not be at all places in an instant, and so the fighter began to falter. Scorched skin from a demon's finger. Acidic agony from a corpse's bite. Bursting breathlessness from a ghoul's kiss.

Muttering incantations, the sorcerer fortified the fighter's strength, summoned winged pixies to beat at the spectres, and called down alternating showers of ice and fire.

The shadows swarmed and drowned the fighter, who lay limp upon the ground, little more than a dark green tunic, indistinguishable in moonlight from the coarse forest grasses.

"Michael!" the sorcerer shouted. "Over here!"

Tempest-quick, a bald cleric appeared. Brown robes clung to him, and an ancient breastplate – engraved with a sun holding a large oak tree in its rays – thudded over his sinewy chest. He gripped a battle axe in both hands. It smoked with supernatural surrender.

Upon seeing the broken form on the ground, he gasped.

Plunging his battle axe into the earth and bending to his knees, Michael stretched his right arm heavenward and pointed his left at the prostrate figure. He chanted in Latin, and a white-blue river of energy coursed from the sky, through his body, and into the unconscious fighter.

"Kate," whispered the sorcerer, stopping his fight to watch the spectacle.

She gasped, drinking in a lungful of air. Blemish-free, she jumped to her feet, short-sword in hand, and resumed slashing at the enemies. "I'm not ready to stay dead yet," she growled.

Michael recovered his sword from the Earth. Standing back-to-back with Kate, they sliced at the hordes while Silvaro continued casting spells. "You never were," he said. "Only God can give back a life from the dead."

Nodding toward the recently deceased creatures stalking their small circle, Kate said, "I'd beg to differ."

"This is no life: only the shadow of it. This is not God."

"You two. Save the theological debates for afterwards," Silvaro said.

Kate jabbed and parried, swung and sliced, anger at her near-defeat punctuating each strike. "There are so many," she panted. "Never seen so many before."

Silvaro handed her a small vial, and she drank it.

Kate's breathing steadied; her muscles stopped burning, and her thoughts focused.

"Michael," Kate said, "your healing power -- it comes from God, right?"

"Aye."

"I said save the religious debates," Silvaro ordered, calling down another shower of ice on the pack of enemies.

"No, wait, I have an idea," Kate said. "The dark hordes are vanishing as soon as they touch our weapons because of the holy water, right?"

"Aye..."

"So they can't touch anything divine – it destroys them. What if you use your healing ability on them?"

"Kate. Oh, naïve, inexperienced Kate. Do you have any idea how ridiculous you sound? I healed myself before I saved you. I can only heal once more before I have to rest: it takes enormous energy. If I use that ability now, I will not be able to help you or Silvaro should you be overcome again."

"But it might work." Kate sliced at another half-dozen figures, and then resumed her defensive position. "Look, there are hundreds of them. How long until you're beaten? Neither Silvaro nor I would be able to help you if you fall."

Michael squinted through midnight's murkiness, seeing no end to the masses. He glanced at Silvaro's silvery face, his gritted teeth, and knew that he would not last much longer. Silvaro was bound in much the same way as Michael: his more impressive abilities required rest and enormous concentration to work. Three times per day, that was all. Already, Silvaro had been reduced to simpler spells that caused only light damage to their enemies and provided some feeble protection for the trio.

"I'll try," he said. "Protect me." He slipped behind Kate, knelt, and called down the blue-white healing waves again.

As Michael directed the pulse towards the unholy throng, the air sizzled with the stench of sulphur and smoke and shadows. Groaning under the strain, he completed a circle and then collapsed, heaving on the ground.

Silence.

Success.

Kate pulled a green bottle from a black silken purse that hung from her waist and handed it to Michael, who drank greedily. She stood, short-sword and shield at the ready, staring at the empty space where the dark horde had loomed moments previously.

"Are you going to live?" she asked.

Michael leaned forward, nodded slowly.

"Good. In that case, I told you so."

***

The trio trudged homeward, Michael insisting that he walk unaided through the knotted trees, over the rugged forest floor. An enormous oak tree, gnarled, weather-beaten, with a trunk as wide as a village church, stretched skyward from the mossy earth. Its chaotic roots grew into a twisted maze, tangling together like cords in careless hands.

Each laid an exhausted right hand upon the colossal trunk, muttered a rhyme in an ancient tongue, and then stepped back, balancing on unsure feet.

The ground yawned, revealing a chasm beneath the tree. They stepped inside, navigating makeshift, mud-born stairs. Once inside the hollow cave, each laid a left hand upon a root, whispered a different charm, and the ground above their heads swallowed.

With a nimble finger, Silvaro sparked life into a pile of dry kindling, and the flames soon danced on the mahogany walls and labyrinthine roots of their sanctuary.

Kate pulled a dagger from one of her many bags, sat near the fire, and began to peel potatoes.

"Oh good," Michael said, leaning against the soft brown wall. "I love it when it's Kate's turn to cook."

Nodding, Silvaro said, "Agreed." He flashed a toothy grin. "Kate, if you wore a dress every once in a while, I'd wife you."

Her laughter was throaty and full. "If you didn't wear a dress, I might take you up on that."

"First, it's not a dress, it's a robe." Silvaro's mocking tone almost – but not quite – masked his petulance. "Second, I've got to keep myself as unencumbered as possible to be able to use the force of this Magicker Oak. The heavier, more constrictive the clothes, the harder it is for me to cast. I actually do my best work completely… skyclad."

Peals of laughter burst forth from Kate as she dropped potatoes into a boiling cauldron. She hardened her face into a mask of sternness. "Don't be disgusting. If you went to fight naked, I might be so overcome with desire that…" The mask broke, and her laughter bubbled forth again.

"I'm sorry; I can't even pretend to finish that seriously." She poked at the vegetable and spice mixture over the fire. "Anyway, Michael wears heavy armour, and he can still do magic."

Still reclining against the cool earthen wall, Michael raised an exhausted eyebrow. "Hold your tongue, harlot," he murmured gently. "My power comes from the divine God in heaven, and so long as He needs me to do His work, He will bless me with His powers. Do not presume to compare His work with this conjurer's cheap tricks." He smiled at Silvaro and closed his eyes.

"Old man, you're just jealous because you're the last of your kind," Silvaro laughed.

Without opening his eyes, Michael said, "King Edwin's Guard has served the Almighty well. We are – we were – the finest legion of holy soldiers trained each generation. God has called my final six brothers and sisters to their eternal reward. Perhaps He will do the same for me when our quest is finished and the final copy of the Daemons' Necronicum has been banished to the hellfires in which it was born."

Stretching, opening his eyes, and sitting forward, Michael removed his breastplate. "But we waste time. For more than a month we have been fighting these skirmishes with constructs and summoned beasts, rather than finding the heart of the darkness. Let us share intelligence. What did you learn from your travels, Silvaro?"

Silvaro shrugged, rubbing heavily scented oils over his sinewy forearms. "Nothing good. The Sons and Daughters of Merlin are struggling. All of the Magicker Oaks except for this one are…inert. Dead. Drained. Powerless."

Kate gaped, stirring the stew. "So all of the sorcerers are…"

"Impotent. Unless they're near this tree, which none of them are, fortunately."

"Why fortunately?" Kate asked. "Surely we could use their help?"

"Even if we had a dozen sorcerers, the power in this Magicker Oak is finite. More sorcerers would mean more power to start off with, then…all spells would fizzle into nothingness when the magic drains away." Silvaro chuckled, a mirthless laugh. He drew his dagger and spun it clumsily around his fingers. "You've seen me with a dagger. Do you really want a group of magicless sorcerers on your side in a fight? Magic's all we have."

"Surely there's more to you than your magic?" Kate said.

"Nope. That's all I ever have been and ever shall be. Just…magic. And a pretty face."

"You forgot – you have your humility." Kate laughed as she ladled steaming stew into three wooden bowls. Exotic spices from faraway lands – cinnamon, hot pepper, turmeric – perfumed the bland root vegetables and sizzled over their tongues, restoring their vitality.

Wiping broth from his chin with the back of his hand, Silvaro joked,

"You sure you're not a sorcerer, Kate? This tastes like witchcraft."

"Ha. And give the Witch-Hunter another reason to pursue me? Being keen with a blade is witchcraft enough, according to him. Would I give him another chance to take from me?"

Michael quenched the ember of Kate's tirade with a patient hand. "In good time, Kate. First we find the book, then we will find the Witch-Hunter and teach him the error of his ways so that he may repent and find God."

"So that he may fall upon my sword and beg for my mercy," Kate growled.

"The rarer action is in virtue, not vengeance," Michael chided, sipping slowly from his bowl. "Everyone knows that witches are not evil – except for him. He can be re-educated, and he can be saved." Michael gestured toward Silvaro's dagger. "Pagan heathen, pass me your weapon."

"Happy to oblige, Christian cabbage-eater." Silvaro passed it over, and Michael doused it in his bottle of holy water.

"What's wrong with cabbage?" Kate asked, balancing a white curly leaf on her spoon.

Scraping the final few drops of stew from his bowl, Michael wiped his mouth neatly on a handkerchief. "We digress. Silvaro, have you found the location of the final book?"

"There is a shrinking circle of wilderness and life. Around the edges is a burnt and blackened earth. It seems that the cancer is spreading inward, toward a centre of evil, likely caused by the book. The animals are missing or silent, as though they have forgotten how to speak – or we have forgotten how to listen."

"You can talk to animals?" Kate asked.

"Of course. Well, I could. Why do you think we eat only vegetables?"

Silvaro said.

"I thought it was because we're renegades who have no money, no sellable skills, and we traded all my jewellery for weapons and supplies. And we don't want to hunt on any lands belonging to King Henry."

"That, too. Though the Young King is the least of our concerns. Anyhow," Silvaro continued, "the centre of the disturbance appears to be at the new Welbeck Abbey. The abbot, Berengar, has been very quiet this past month, and the rumour is that he sent all of his monks away on various charitable missions."

"It is unusual that he has sent everyone away. It is possible that he has taken possession of the book – and the book has, in turn, taken possession of him," Michael mused. "We go at dawn. Welbeck Abbey is a three-hour walk from here. If we attack at noon, his power will be at its lowest ebb: black magic works best at midnight."

"Now who's a pagan heathen?" Silvaro joked. "Seems you know a lot about demons for a priest, old man."

A plaintive smile painted Michael's ageless face. "You have no idea how old I truly am." At Silvaro's quizzical look, Michael chuckled. "Do you recall, back in the year 1000, when it was the End of Days, and all life ceased?"

Silvaro scoffed. "That was over a hundred and fifty years ago. And of course the world didn't end."

Stretching and pulling a rough burlap blanket over himself, Michael said, "Of course it didn't. You are welcome for that. Now, get some rest."

***

Autumn's grey-blue chill iced the air. Welbeck Abbey squatted, stout and square, over the brown-green grass.

The heaven-bent trio knelt, nervous, on the bank of a murky lake, chewing at hunks of rye bread that rasped bitterly across their tongues. The purses about their waists were laden with potions to improve strength and concentration, heal wounds, add dexterity, dispel disease, hasten their reflexes – anything that might give them an advantage over their unseen enemy.

Michael held his palms upwards toward the heavens in silent prayer. A hundred yards away, Silvaro meditated, drinking in the rough grasses, the smoky, hovering clouds, the hushed rustle of blackbirds and crows in the trees, the whisper of the northern winds.

Kate stretched her muscles and stared silently at her short sword, balancing it on her palm, flipping it, spinning it, contemplating the sharpness of the blade.

Michael mouthed a silent “Amen” and regarded Kate warmly. “You have no need to be nervous,” he said.

“I’m not nervous. I just haven’t done this. Gone on the offensive, I mean. I don’t know what to expect. The fights we’ve had with this person’s spells have been bad enough.” She gripped the handle of her blade in white knuckles.

Michael’s gentle smile calmed Kate, and she replaced the sword in its scabbard. “When Peter died while destroying the last Book and left me the last of my kind, I feared that all was lost. That was the only time my faith in the Almighty has ever trembled.” His voice, honeyed and mellow, stained with shame. “But I was wrong.”

Kate squinted at Michael. “What restored your faith?”

“You.”

She laughed and studied the gathering tabby-cat clouds. “Me?”

“You.” Michael put a comforting arm around Kate’s shoulders. “I had just buried Peter, my oldest and dearest friend. Wandering through the lonely woods, trying to find my way back to Silvaro's Magicker Oak, a wild hellcat attacked me."

Kate's eyes widened.

Michael laughed. "You," he said. Then, chuckling, "Please, I mean no offence. Your hissing, spitting, growling, the way your blade seemed to be everywhere at once, like a cat's claws – in my mind you were a hellcat." He shifted into a seated position, facing Kate. "You nearly bested me in battle..."

"I thought you were going to attack me."

"... and I have exponentially more experience than you. Oh, Kate, I don't begrudge you your attack on me. When our fight had finished and I realised that you were no more than a kitten with her tail caught in a trapper's snare, it was then that I knew that God had a plan. He took Peter from me... but He sent me you instead." Michael cupped Kate's jaw tenderly in the palm of his hand, which was surprisingly warm and smooth, despite the long years it had spent wielding a battle axe. "You have a purpose here. Your hand – and your path – is guided by God."

Silvaro's shadow dimmed the noontide sun. "Moving in on my future wife, Michael?" he joked.

"I'm not marrying either of you."

"Just a bit of...fatherly advice. Heavenly Father, of course. I'm far too old to be Kate's father," Michael winked.

"You two ready? It's time," Silvaro said.

Kate and Michael stood, brushed themselves off, and readied their weapons. Silvaro cast a stealth shield on the trio, a trick which meant that, as long as they remained silent, anyone who happened to glance at them would immediately find his attention drawn away, forgetting in an instant what had been seen.

Skirting around the edge of the building, the group found an open entrance and slipped inside.

The smell of sulphur drew them to their destination: the refectory.

As they slid through the archway, they spied a portly man, with hair like mouldy straw traversing the room, his bulbous nose stuck in a book. Red cord stitched the vellum in place and the covers were made of leather so black that they seemed to drink in the raging firelight.

"Witch-Hunter!" Kate's shriek dispelled her stealth charm, and she charged at the man, her sword held high above her head, her years of secret training forgotten, fuelled only by desperate, desperate hatred.

"Kate, no!" Silvaro cried, similarly dismissing his charm. As the Witch-Hunter drew breath to mutter an incantation, Silvaro stretched his arm out toward the man. "You are spell-stopped!"

The Witch-Hunter halted in place, a black tuft of air hovering on the palm of his hand. His snake-like lips froze in a hideous sneer. Silvaro grasped Kate's wrist in his hand and pulled her back.

"How long will he stay like that?" Kate asked.

"Three minutes, at most."

"That's two and a half minutes more than I need." Wrenching her wrist free from the sorcerer's fingers, Kate tore toward the immobile man, her sword in front of her, ready to cut his heart in two, the way he had cut hers.

"Kate, no!" Silvaro insisted. "If you touch him, you'll be frozen too. And he can hear and see everything; he just can't move."

Kate skittered to a stop, circling the man as a wolf circles an injured deer, twirling her sword around in circles near her hip. "Malcolm." Her voice dripped with disgust. "You repulsive creature. Was it not enough, was it not enough that you killed Thomas, a sweet, beloved boy who had never even touched a sword? No. You then spread rumours that I had killed him, my only brother, so that I could change the laws and inherit my father's lands!"

Kate trembled, her words half-growled, half-shrieked. "Are you so sure that I am a witch that you would travel hundreds of miles just to find me? You're so certain that you are doing God's work, that you would take an innocent life, persecute an innocent woman. Look into your black heart and tell me, honestly – is this what you believe your God would want?"

A finger on Malcolm's outstretched hand twitched. The black plumes quivered.

"Kate…" warned Silvaro.

Kate stepped backward and assumed an offensive stance, ready to attack the moment the spell broke.

"And now you're here," she continued, "with the final copy – reading the final copy – of the Daemon's Necronicum. A man of God so pure that he murders children and frames an innocent woman, and calls it holy work. Now who's in league with the devil? Now who's the witch?"

The wisps of black air churned in Malcolm's hand, slowly, as though fighting their way through lard.

Malcolm spoke for the first time since the band had arrived. His speech was slow and stilted, as though he were shouting under water. "To…fight…evil…one…must…understand…evil." The whirling ball in Malcolm's hand gathered speed, as though moving through honey now, rather than lard. "Pray, Witch-Hunter, in this, the moment of your death. God might forgive you - but I won't."

Turning to Silvaro, deliberately ignoring the still-stealthy Michael, Kate said, "The Witch-Hunter is mine. No one interferes.

Understood?"

Silvaro began to protest, but was stopped by a hand on his arm. "Yes, Kate. But help is here if you need it."

The spell holding Malcolm in place broke. From the palm of his hand sprang six shadows. Kate's weapon sliced through the nearest like smoke.

"One day, they'll see I'm right," Malcolm growled, conjuring more shadows as Kate cut her way through the summoned figures. "Everyone will know that witches come from the devil, and your kind will be punished. You won't drag any more souls to Hell with you."

"My brother..." Kate began, jabbing at a shadow.

"I saved your brother's soul. His life was cut short, but you'd have corrupted him if he had lived any longer. Better a short life on Earth and an eternity in Heaven than a long life and an eternity of torment."

Kate rushed forward, her sword held out in front of her, ignoring the insubstantial black masses that seethed from the Witch-Hunter's palms and hissed at her skin. The potions and spells that charmed her absorbed most of the damage but began to chafe away. Each blow from the shadows bruised a little more, scratched a little more deeply, ripped a little more sharply. A sickly smile invaded the right side of Malcolm's face. Too late, Kate skidded, trying to stop her forward movement, her eyes widening. A thick snake made of smoking leather ripped away from the wall, wrapped itself around her right arm, and twisted, burning her, dragging her forward toward the fire, using her momentum from her earlier attack. She cried out, dropping her sword as her shoulder dislocated. Picking it up with her left hand, she began to hack at the cursed object.

"Left-handed!" proclaimed Malcolm. "I said you were a witch." He turned to Silvaro. "Didn't I say she was a witch?"

Kate was dragged closer to the sulphurous fire, writhing and chopping at the snake.

Silvaro's face crumpled. His heart beat wildly, a caged hawk desperate to escape. "I'm sorry, Kate," he said and turned his palms skyward. A raincloud began to gather inside the refectory.

"No!" Kate shouted, still struggling. "You can't put the fire out; we have to use it to destroy the book!"

Silvaro clapped his hands and the cloud disappeared. Instead, he conjured a whip made of ice and flung it toward the snake. Halfway across its trajectory, the whip disappeared. Desperately, he cast an immobilising spell on the snake; a web should have appeared, wrapping itself around the target and pinning it to the ground. Of course, Kate would be trapped too, but it would stop her inexorable, inevitable, pull toward the fire. The web did not appear. Frantically, futilely, Silvaro ran through a chain of spells, starting with more powerful conjurations and running down to simple fireballs and iceballs. Each fizzled.

Malcolm's laugh slithered through the air, high and spindly. "Your pagan magic fails you, sorcerer. Have you used up all the power in that Magicker Oak of yours?" He rubbed his hands together and advanced on the sorcerer.

A battle axe lodged itself in Malcolm's back. The snake flopped to the ground, limp, a decorative piece once more.

"No!" Kate shrieked. "I said he was mine!"

Michael spoke, dispelling his stealth. "Yes. You could have fought him in the life-after-life."

"Michael, what took you so long?" Silvaro asked.

"Respecting Kate's wishes. Analysing the Witch-Hunter for signs that he could be redeemed. His decision to study the book rather than to destroy it was his undoing – and the reason for your brother's death, Kate. At his core, Malcolm was not evil. He was simply weak. Once, after all, he was a man of God."

Kate spat on the corpse. "God can have him. Or the devil."

The three gathered at a heavy table near the fire. Michael laid the final copy of the cursed book upon it. Silvaro rubbed his hands together and muttered a simple incantation that should have levitated the book.

Nothing happened.

His face crumpled. "I thought it might have been the Witch-Hunter blocking my spells. It wasn't. There really is no more magic." He traced the outline of the oak tree on his robe wistfully. "All my life I've been a sorcerer. I'm not even Silvaro any more. Just plain old Alexander. What am I going to do now? What else can I be?"

Placing a hand on Silvaro's shoulder, Michael said, "A good man."

Michael closed his eyes and muttered in Latin, sprinkling droplets of holy water over the book. The pages smoked and sizzled, a wailing sound as though the pages themselves bemoaned their own death. Silvaro (no, no longer Silvaro, now just plain Alexander) and Kate watched silently.

"And now we bestow the book back to the fires in which it was born. Thus ends the reign of black magic."

A hand slammed down onto the open pages. "No."

Michael's eyes snapped open and he stared at Silvaro. "My friend, what do you...?"

"No." Silvaro snatched the book towards him, picked it up, and cradled it against his chest. "There's no more magic in this world except for what is written in this book. It's mine. It was destiny that I find it. I can study it, control it, and wield the magic described in it myself. Others failed because they were weak, but I'm strong. I don't have to lose my sorcery. I don't have to lose myself."

Michael's hand went to his weapon. He did not draw it but kept his grip tight on the handle. Kate watched Michael and did the same with her left hand, her right arm dangling uselessly by her side.

"Silvaro." Michael's voice was gentle, as though approaching a nervous, dangerous animal. "This is not you. This is the book. Do not be drawn in by its deception. Give me the book, friend, that we may end this journey."

Silvaro gripped the book more tightly. He stared at the pages, studied Michael's imploring face, and then he looked back at the book.

Snake-quick, Silvaro's dagger sliced into the gap in Michael's armour, between his neck plate and breast plate, piercing his collarbone.

Michael's mouth fell open, and he let out a cry of pain. Momentarily, Silvaro stared in horror at his hand, his dagger, then at his victim's face. The dagger smoked and sizzled in his hand, and he dropped the weapon as though he had burnt his palm. Jerking his hand away, he wrapped both arms around the book, shook his head, turned, and ran out of the refectory.

As he sank onto the rocky floor, Michael knelt. He stretched one arm skyward, blinking back the pain from his wound, and aimed the other at Kate.

"No!" Kate shouted. "Michael, what are you doing? Heal yourself first!"

Waves of blue light washed over the fighter. Her arm snapped back into place; black bruises and angry red burns melted into snowy skin, and the ringing in her ears quietened to an eerie silence.

"Go!" Michael ordered. "Stop him, or this will have been for nothing."

Fleet and fierce, Kate flew out of the refectory, the pads of her feet pounding the hard stone. From the potions around her waist, she grabbed two at random and gulped them down, throwing the bottles behind her. They clattered against the floor.

Exploding out into the cool autumn afternoon, Kate stopped, searching for Silvaro like a cat hunts a bird. Silence. The birds and other wildlife were mute. Even the wind stopped rustling in the trees.

"Silvaro!" Kate demanded. Then, she took a deep breath, closed her eyes, and listened to the wise voice deep inside of herself. One of the potions must have enhanced my wisdom, she thought. "Silvaro, please come out. I understand how you feel." Silence. "Silvaro, please. I know what it means to lose yourself - your identity, your whole existence..." She put her sword back in her scabbard and raised her left hand above her head, careful to dangle her right as though it was still injured. "You're probably feeling very scared, and very alone. That's completely understandable."

A rustle came from a shrubbery, behind and to the right of her. She attuned to it, marked in her mind's eye where the disturbance lay, and made no indication that she had heard it.

"I was going to be Lady Katherine of Kent. I had a loving family, a wonderful life, and an indulgent father who let my brother sew and knit while he let me train in swordplay. I would have had wealth, freedom, and all my heart desired." Another rustle from the same location.

"That was stolen from me. Just as your destiny – Silvaro the Sorcerer, Master of the Arcane – was stolen from you." She paused, lowered her left hand to her hip, her right hand hovering just above her weapon. "I, too, have had my purpose stolen from me: I no longer need to seek revenge for my brother's death. We are one and the same: purposeless, our destinies fulfilled. We must make a choice now. We can lament the void that stands before us, or we can embrace the freedom it gives us." The rustles were closer now, almost directly behind Kate.

"I'm no longer Lady Katherine. Just Kate, Kate the rogue, Kate the renegade. And I love it. As happy as I would have been as Lady Katherine, I love being just plain Kate even more. In time, Silvaro, you will lay your chosen name to rest and will embrace being Alexander. Please, Silvaro. Let me help you."

Thin and pale, Silvaro emerged from the bushes, clutching the book to his chest with white knuckles. Kate turned around slowly, studying his facial expressions, his stance, his hands and feet, calculating his next move. "You are so beautiful in the autumn sunlight," he said. "I never realised before."

Charisma. That must have been the other potion, Kate thought. Well, it won't hurt.

Stepping towards him, her left arm outstretched, Kate forced a smile and said, "I know you are a good person at heart. You know what needs to happen. You're scared right now. Impotent. That will pass. And you'll be the person who rid the world from evil." To emphasise her final sentence, she caressed Silvaro's shoulder.

Silvaro put his hand over Kate's, his grip on the book loosening. He blinked slowly, took a deep breath, and raised his gaze to meet hers.

Suddenly, his soft mouth contorted into a snarl. His grip on Kate's hand tightened, and he twisted her arm behind her back. "A charisma charm?" he sneered. "Did you really think I wouldn't notice?"

Kate drew her weapon with her right hand and rammed the hilt of it into Silvaro's side, just under his ribcage. Winded by the blow, he dropped her arm and doubled over. Spinning around, she thrust the heel of her hand into his nose, and, while he was stunned, brought the hilt of her sword down over his head. He fell sideways to the ground with a thump.

Whip-quick, Kate grabbed the book and pounded her way back to the refectory. Without opening it, without even glancing at its cover, she threw the book into the fire and stoked the coals. A terrible hissing screamed through the air. Sparks glowed red, and the smell of sulphur snaked through the room. In seconds, the pages burned into nothingness. The covers began to char and curl inward.

The spectacle over, Kate dashed to Michael's side. He lay on the stony floor, his armour awkwardly balancing his body. She removed his helmet, crossed her legs, and laid his head in her lap. His heaven-blue eyes faded to a dull, slate grey and struggled to focus on Kate's face.

Footsteps drummed ominously along the stones. Kate gripped her sword and held it out in front of her, but did not move. "Don't come any closer, Silvaro. You've done enough."

"Alexander." The ex-sorcerer put his hands up and indicated the dagger – his one weapon – lying useless on the floor near Michael's body. "Silvaro died when the magic died." He advanced slowly toward Kate and Michael. Kate drew back her weapon, but Michael waved a weak hand, and she laid it on the floor next to her. Silvaro – now Alexander – knelt at Michael's feet. "Michael," he said. "Words cannot express my regret for…"

"My friend," Michael interrupted., "your actions were not your own. These books defended themselves: they latched on to human souls and corrupted them. The devil is clever indeed. Why do you think we always travel in threes? If one is corrupted, the other two can stop him. Why do you think I have lost my final six brothers and sisters in the long journey to destroy these books?"

Kate stroked Michael's chin and loosened his breastplate. "Then you came here knowing that you would probably die."

"Kate, I came here knowing that I would die. God's purpose for me is no longer. I will finally rest, now that the world is safe from evil.

Alexander grasped Michael's ankle in earnest. "Still, I am so sorry for being so weak that I..."

"Accepted," Michael said. "You are forgiven."

Wiping a tear from her cheek, Kate said, "Oh, Michael, this is all my fault. If I hadn't been so obsessed with the Witch-Hunter..."

"You, too, are forgiven." Michael coughed, weakly wiping blood away from his blue mouth.

Kate gasped. "Wait! You don't have to give your life for this, Michael. Why haven't you healed yourself? You only used your power once."

"Divine healing only works on injuries inflicted by an enemy. They are powerless against wounds given in betrayal. I have been keeping myself alive through the pagan potions" – he winked at Alexander – "but they are not enough. Soon, I will join my brothers, my earthly king, and my heavenly King."

He drew a rasping breath. "Please, lay me to rest in the village that bears my beloved King Edwin's name, that I may serve him in death as I served him in life."

Kate's eyebrow raised. "You actually served King Edwin? You weren't just part of some sect that used his name?"

"I said I was old." Michael gripped Kate's hand. "And now I will see my beloved king and my beloved Marian again, after all these years."

"Marian," Kate said. "That's a lovely name. If I ever have a daughter, I'll call her Marian – or Michael, if I have a son."

"That is the greatest honour I could hope for."

Michael closed his eyes for the last time.

***

Alexander leaned against the rough tree that had sheltered them in the weeks leading up to their final battle. A deep chasm in the ground yawned, not from the tree's magic, but from the shovels the pair had borrowed from Welbeck Abbey.

Reverently, the pair lowered their friend's body into the ground and filled in the earth. Neither spoke for several minutes.

Kate laid a smooth palm against the tree's huge, knotted trunk. "Good-bye, Magicker Oak," she said. "You served us well."

"It's not a Magicker Oak any more," Alexander said. "Just a big oak tree."

"A Major Oak."

"Yes."

The wind whispered in the trees as the sun sank below the horizon.

Alexander's awkward laugh broke the silence. "I'll still wife you, if you put on a dress."

"We both know that's not going to happen." Kate sighed. "We need to find Berengar and the monks, let them know they can come back to the abbey. Who knows where Malcolm sent them?"

Staring up at the leaves, ignoring Kate, Alexander asked, "How will we live in a world without magic? In a world where the animals are voiceless?"

"It is a brave new world. Humanity is innovative and resilient. We will find a way," Kate reassured him. "And there was a magic in Michael beyond what either of us can understand. Perhaps – when this tree grows strong again – magic will return to our land."

PAUL JAMESON

ILLUSTRATIONS BY TREVOR CROOK

ERIC AND OSCAR

I have always liked history, particularly the ancient battles, and an article, *Did a King Die at Cuckney?*, blogged on the *Our Nottinghamshire* website caught my attention.

There was also a plea from a like-minded history buff appealing for others to join him in researching this mystery. So, the Battle of Hatfield Investigation Society was born, and I have been Chairman for the past two years.

The Society has, over the last four years, considered the evidence that King Edwin of Northumbria's last battle may have taken place near Cuckney. The story is at times complicated and confusing, even for adults, but as a time-travelling story of a modern-day dad and his lad, it encourages children to think of the distant past and make history a reality. Young boys would have fought alongside their fathers, brothers and even grandfathers in battles long ago.

Our local schools, Cuckney and Meden, have been engaged in the project with us, and loved the excitement of such an important battle taking place almost on their doorstep.

Anglo-Saxon battlefields are almost impossible to locate and it will take time, funding and good luck for this project to discover the truth behind the mass burial pit found (almost by accident) under St Mary's at Cuckney in 1950. The Society has come a long way since 2013, and is now poised on the brink of the next phase of archaeology – to excavate and date a large re-burial pit in the modern graveyard.

ERIC AND OSCAR

The story of the Battle of Hatfield that may have happened in Bassetlaw more than 1000 years ago.

"H'm," said Dad.

Oh no! I thought. Something is coming I don't want to hear, see or do.

"You know that game you're always playing, and you have to go out of the house with your mobile and follow a map to catch a little cartoon thing?"

"Er, Dad, I've not played that for ages."

"Well, good. I'm pleased you have seen the error of your ways and now we can do something useful together, you know 'dads and lads'."

"Well, what's that, then?" I asked.

"How about a battle re-enactment?"

I went quiet. I had visions of dressing-up clothes, tents, mud and camp fires. No, no, this is not me!

We were just passing the church and Dad steered me in that direction. "It's time for me to tell you a story, Oscar," Dad said. I put on my interested face and switched off my brain.

"Long, long ago, in a time they called the 'Dark Ages', there was a

King called Edwin…"

I felt a sudden chill and the wind swirled around me.

"Dad, I don't have time to listen to stupid, boring stories. Can't you just leave me alone?"

A horrible nightmare feeling was rising in me, turning everything around to darkness, I felt heavy as if I couldn't move

But I knew Dad wouldn't let me go until he had told his story.

"Before this was a village with roads and cars, it was a green place. Trees covered every hill and bordered every path; they shaded every stream and this was a kingdom."

"What, here?" I said. "We don't have a kingdom around here; we don't even have a takeaway!" I turned away, hopefully, to make a quick getaway.

Dad was insistent. "This was a kingdom with a king."

"Well, who was that then?" I said.

"His name was Penda and this kingdom was called Mercia, and in those dark days they had to watch their backs because there was always someone waiting for a chance to take over."

"Do you mean a battle, Dad?"

He nodded. This story was getting better!

"In those days, a twelve-year-old like you, Oscar, would have had to fight for the king and revenge his killers if he died. These battles secured the kingdom's borders and brought peace to the land, but victory came at a price and one by one the kings were killed until there was only one great king left."

"Who was that, then, Dad?"

"His name was Raedwald."

“Oh, I know him, Dad. He was buried in a ship with lots of gold, but who was the king who fought our Penda?”

“Well, there were three: Edwin and his son Prince Osfrith, from Northumberland, our Penda of Mercia and Cadwallon, from Wales.”

“Wow, it must have been a big battle, Dad.”

“It was. lots of men died. In fact, not so many years ago, some workmen were digging in our church and found a burial pit full of skeletons.”

Now I was interested! “How many, Dad?”

“Well, some said more than two hundred skeletons, and they were all men.”

I wondered how they knew that, but I thought I would look it up on the internet later. Dad told me the battle would be fought on foot

and a fight to the death, the bloodiest battle you would ever see.

"Was there a princess, Dad? These kinds of stories always have stupid kings falling in in love." I started walking back to our house. Hm, and just as I was beginning to think this was going to be a good story!

With one swift movement, Dad grabbed my arm and turned me round. "Let me finish, Oscar." Dad told me that they had also found a lead coffin in the church, and when they prised open the lid there was a beautiful girl with red hair lying in it. In a few moments, she melted away and there was just dust left in the bottom of the coffin.

"Oh, Dad, was there blood?"

I felt the wind roaring and the ground shaking and held tight to Dad's hand.

Someone was calling my name, **Osfrith, Osfrith...**

Penda ran towards the approaching soldiers and sought out their leader.

"The rumours are true then, Cadwallon. Edwin is advancing from the north."

"How many day's march until we meet?" said Cadwallon. "And is that evil dog Lord Godbold in his company?"

Penda shook his head. "My man has calculated three days hence, but Edwin will take to the high ground and hope to surprise us."

"Ah, yes, but he does not know that we march together," said Cadwallon.

"Osfrith, you sleep like the dead. Wake up, my son," said Edwin. Sleep and dreams were holding me so tightly; no, I cannot wake, but Father was insistent. "I will not ask thee again, my Prince. We must make ready now."

I pulled myself up by the cross Paulinus, the preacher from Rome, had given to Father when he was made a Christian. He always wore it around his neck. "You mean we will make the battle today?" I asked.

"It is difficult to say, my son. Our spies have not returned to me." Edwin began to move away.

"Father, never have I seen greater among men than you, a noble warrior in the far front of the battle."

"So love me, my dear son, and follow me."

"Father, kings are to be feared, not loved. We laughed together and walked back to the cover of the trees.

So, the battle lines were drawn, and we were waiting on a densely wooded hill, and we could hear the rhythm of many a hundred men as they marched below us. Father, the King, had made a stirring battle speech, and the men had made ready with close shield walls. I looked at my sword, so precious; the blacksmith had taken hours to craft it in a red-hot fire, twisting the iron rods together and then hammering it to shape. I wondered how much blood there would be on it by the end of the day.

As soon as the battle cry was raised we came forward in our war dress of chainmail shirts, carrying long spears and the great war shields. It was easy for us: we were on the top of the hill, but it was hard to see the enemy through the trees. We held them for many an hour, but it was a larger army than we had expected. Had Cadwallon met with Penda? Father gave the signal to his men to command 'retrench', and we started to back down the hill. Our front line held, but we were slowly, slowly retreating down the north side of the hill. As we came out of the trees, the enemy were above us and I could see the blood-lust in their eyes. Father ordered the shield wall to part and the javelin throwers came forward, but it was hard for them to throw uphill. Our men were falling all around me, and as the enemy advanced it became a killing ground. But we held firm, covering our heads with our shields as our archers delivered a rain of arrows into the front ranks of the enemy. We threw rocks, spears, axes – anything to break their resolve. There was pushing, yelling and blood – so much blood. It became a field of hell. There was nowhere for us to go, just slowly, slowly down the hill towards the river; we could not know it would stop our retreat. I saw my father fall and a great cry went up from the enemy. I could not get to him; that bold heart, had it stopped beating? I stepped over the bodies and detritus of war to hold his hand. There is no glory of war when you have lost that most dear to you. As I kissed his face and held him in my arms reddened with his gore, I felt a sharp pain and

I heard the wind roaring and the ground *Shaking*.

Someone was calling my name, **Oscar, Oscar…**

It was Dad. I opened my eyes and looked at his familiar face.

"Come on, lad, wake up," Dad said. "You tripped and banged your head on that metal thing sticking out of the ground."

I carefully sat up with Dad's help and looked around. Dad had, with difficulty, pulled the 'thing' out of the ground; it was an old sword pommel.

"We had better get this checked out," Dad said.

"Let's go home. All this has been too much for me today," I said. "Oh, what are we checking out, this metal thing or me?"

Dad gave me a funny look. "Love you, Oscar."

"And I love you, Dad."

EPILOGUE

"H'm," said Dad. "Here we are again, Oscar."

Well, how the years have flown! I remember that day as if it were yesterday. Was it the bump on the head, or did I travel back in time and fight in a battle with King Edwin, who looked remarkably like Dad? He is an old man now but still tells me stories. Are they true, or is he a good storyteller?

His story of the battle made me curious to discover the truth and this steered me into a career in what Dad calls 'archae-whatsit'. After my time at university, I came back to live with Dad; Mum had died and he was on his own.

Dad was telling me today of a website called the Battle of Hatfield Investigation Society, who were to try to find out if the skeletons were the lost armies of Edwin, Penda and Cadwallon. Dad has repeated the story many times of the need to extend coal mining under our church in the 1950s, and how it was strengthened by using reinforced concrete. Under the church floor the workmen found a burial pit full of skeletons. Dad said he had heard they were in deep layers of three with their feet pointing to the east, so people thought it might be a sort of Christian burial. The bodies disappeared out of sight under the north wall of the church, so they must have been there before our church was built in the 12th century. Dad knew someone called Alan, who, as a choirboy, had seen about twenty skulls displayed on a windowsill in the church, looked at them and realised all had pick-type damage, perhaps to make sure they were dead before burial.

Mr Barley, an archaeologist, came to have a look around and talk to the Vicar and the workmen. They were going to have some of the bones examined by an expert, but this all fell through. So, he wrote an article instead and the bodies were reburied somewhere in the churchyard and forgotten. Another man, called Mr Revill, visited twenty-four years later and wrote another article, but this time he suggested that our village, or near about, could have been the site of the Battle of Hatfield, but still nothing was resolved.

Lots of people have asked why these two important men in the field of archaeology didn't search further for the answer, but, in those days, a career in archaeology was unusual, and the television programme called 'Time Team' had not been invented – or the words 'geophys' and 'anomaly'. After all, it was only a few years after the end of the Second World War and there was lots of rebuilding to do after the bombing. Mr Barley was kept very busy trying to save many of the old medieval buildings from the new ringroads. He didn't have time to think about the band of brothers under the church. Someone asked him, many years later, if he regretted anything he had left unfinished. "Yes," he said, "the bodies under the church – I wish I had found out who they were."

In the thirteenth year of the millennium, the Battle Society was formed in our village and it caused quite a bit of excitement. Some people were for and some people against; it was like a battle all over again. Gradually things settled down and they began to kick ideas around. It was decided, with the help of an archaeology company and a questionnaire sent around the outlying villages, to choose five topics for investigation. These were the little Castle Hill, our church, a local gentleman's photo collection, local buildings, field and street names and, most important, the skeletons discovered in 1950/51.

Well, by the time they had sorted things out two years had passed by, but one day in November 2015 things were buzzing. Vans and trailers were unloaded; people were milling around, but gradually order reigned and things began to happen. Dad and I walked down to the site and started chatting to two young men who were using GPR in the graveyard.

"Have you found anything?" Dad asked.

"Well, yes. Just found a hot spot!" Matt said.

Oh, it was right next to a fresh grave that had been opened for a burial that very day. Could this be the re-burial pit from 1951? Just then the church clock began to strike the hour. It was 12 o'clock, but it struck thirteen, just as it had all those years ago.

I heard the wind roaring and the ground shaking…

The Battle of Hatfield Investigation Society are continuing their search for the truth behind the mass grave found under Cuckney Church in 1950.

MANDY COGGAN

THE SHERWOOD STRANGER

Mandy is a keen reader rather than a writer but was honoured to win last year's competition.

She particularly enjoys non-fiction books and likes to widen her knowledge about true events and acts of heroism. She lives in Bassetlaw with her cat and has two grown up children.

When she is not reading, Mandy enjoys crafts and being out and about in the countryside.

She likes to travel and enjoys being in the company of others.

When travelling alone, she likes to sample local culture and 'people-watch' in a cosy cafe with a book and a latte. Hopefully you will enjoy her story over a cuppa, too.

THE SHERWOOD STRANGER

He stepped off the train onto the platform and was almost swept away by the rush-hour throng of Friday morning commuters eager to get to work, eager to meet deadlines before doing the same journey in reverse. From beneath his cap, tilted to one side, he peered at them scornfully, bewildered at their determination and pace. Like ants on the forest floor, he thought to himself. He was looking for the Law Courts, a somewhat impressive building with a glass atrium (so he was told) close to Nottingham rail station. "How does one get to the other side of this road?" he pondered as he stood watching the endless streams of traffic. Finally he made a break for it, his heeled boots stomping and his long coat-tails flapping, as he ran desperately to the other side. Horns blasted and drivers shouted profanities as he very nearly caused a collision. "Bloody idiot!" called the bus driver as he leaned out of his window, waving in the direction of the strangely dressed man.

OK, so he was perhaps a little odd looking for the twenty-first century, but are we not a little more broadminded in our acceptance of others? It is no longer a shock to see a man who is dressed somewhat flamboyantly, let alone a man with long hair. Perhaps so, but this man was no liberal thinker, either. He almost barged two suited men into the canal as they embraced, exchanging a peck on the cheek, vowing to meet up later for lunch.

"Hey, don't mind me!" called one man, rubbing the dirt from his sleeve, while his companion lovingly straightened out the creases.

The strange man scowled and spat in disgust as he pushed his way past them along the towpath. He muttered something inaudible to himself and then turned back to check he really had seen two men embracing together in broad daylight.

"No harm done – just ignore him," said his friend, hoping there wasn't going to be an altercation.

"You're right," he replied. "See you about one-ish for lunch!"

On reaching the building which he assumed was the Law Courts, the man stopped dead in his tracks, causing a nearby cyclist to suddenly brake and swerve around him. Unfortunately, he hit a stone and was catapulted from his bike to the floor. Two women immediately leapt from a bench to his aid, helping him stand and checking his minor injuries. Perhaps this was a trick he could use himself if it meant that two fine ladies came to your immediate assistance! While they fussed around the cyclist and dabbed his injuries with clean tissues, the man glanced down at the bike and was not sure if it was a worthy asset to steal. He picked up the bike, surprisingly lighter than he had anticipated, and examined it carefully. The crossbar seemed uncomfortably high and the handlebars coiled like rams horns must certainly make it difficult to ride. It would mean him having to arch his back in a crouched position, and goodness knows how he would prevent his coat from getting entangled in the chain. He thought better of it and dropped it back down with a thud. The cyclist was shocked, yet relieved to see his bike still in one piece, and not about to be stolen by the strange man. The ladies were not as ladylike as he had originally thought. "Perhaps if you cut your hair you might be able to see where you are going, you stupid man!" called one of them.

Taking a piece of crumpled paper from his breast pocket, he glanced at the building and then back to the paper, not sure if he had arrived at his destination. He moved closer to the glass front of the building and was about to enter when he recoiled in panic. Two men in official uniform were approaching each person as they entered the building, searching their clothing and passing their bags through scanning devices. Subconsciously, he felt the blade of his knife against his skin in his boot. One of the men with a balding head saw the curious stranger and, sensing something was wrong, he came out.

"Can I help you, sir?" he asked, eyeing the rather eccentric-looking man up and down.

He thrust his papers into the official's hand and waited for his response. He reminded him of somebody he had once been acquainted with, but he couldn't quite place him. He looked at his rather rotund stomach and receding hairline, but it had been some years now.

"Some map you have here, sir!" said the security guard and then reeled in horror at what he then read. "I'm afraid this court does not deal with that sort of crime, sir. You'll be wanting the Crown Court, not the Magistrates' Court, and that'll be back over the main road and right onto Canal Street. It says you're to be there at 3pm; that's plenty of time. We don't normally let the press in until half an hour before."

After handing back the paper, the security guard hurried back to his colleague, desperate to share his news. "He must be some kind of journalist or undercover reporter... ," whispered Frank to William, who was handing a rucksack back to its owner "... and I bet you the place will be snided-out with camera crews."

They were both due to finish their shifts at 1pm, so an extra few hours watching the drama unfold in Courtroom 1 seemed like a rather interesting piece of overtime. "This is going to be some case, Will, let me tell you! Although how on earth he got to find out is beyond me, when we actually work for the courts!"

Will looked out towards the stranger and thought he knew him. He saw so many people working here, it would be hard to place him and there were no other men like him on the staff rota. Perhaps he had seen him in the village. There were always tourists passing through, eager to soak up the local history. He awkwardly looked away as the stranger tilted his cap and then turned.

The stranger crossed over the canal bridge to rows of tables assembled outside bars, stretching right up to the water's edge.

Sitting down, he pulled out a newspaper from a nearby bin and began to scour its contents. May 23rd 2017. The sickening headlines glared out at him: 'At least 22 innocent people dead including children, following a confirmed terrorist attack in Manchester'; 'The perpetrator thought to be radicalised perhaps by social media giants whom seem untouchable by the law...'

Confused as to what social media was, he turned the pages and read equally disturbing news items: President Putin of Russian had equipped his army with nuclear ballistic missiles capable of destroying small counties... Mustard gas attacks in Syria... Local thug stabs shop keeper and steals cigarettes... US president still wanting a wall to keep Mexicans out... Man recruits five teenagers and kills love rival before dumping body in wasteland...

" We're not open yet !" called a man from the nearby bar, which was his cue to move on.

He tossed the paper back into the bin and hoped to find something more uplifting to pass the time. He glanced up high on Carrington Street: the beautiful arched windows above the many shops and eateries and the Gresham Hotel and wondered who might frequent such grand buildings. He was sure that he had never been in such buildings, yet they appeared to be seeped in history. He imagined them hosting prestigious parties, attended by glamorous ladies and gentlemen far more noble and superior than himself. It was then that his eye caught a sign and he knew straightaway that this was one establishment that he had frequented. 'Nottingham Castle', the sign read, and a warm glow immediately enveloped him.

With a renewed skip in his step, our curious gentleman followed the street signs and quickly found himself on Castle Road looking for a break in the high stone walls that stood defiantly on the sandstone rocks and grassy verge. It seemed impermeable back then, but even more so today. His skills in breaking and entering had become somewhat rusty. There was a time when a portcullis would not have deterred him, let alone a ten-foot wall. He came to Lenton Road and found an entrance, surprised to see several other people also making their way towards the castle. Following the throng, he was somewhat taken back when an elderly man asked him for a ticket. Normally he would have brushed him aside, but today he was determined to make the right impression. "Ticket?" he asked. "Whatever for? Richard has never asked me for a ticket!" The elderly man went to speak to his superior and within a few moments he returned.

"Richard is not in today, sir, but my boss says on this occasion you can go through but remember your pass next time, please. The lesson is taking place in the Long Gallery next to the library."

He nodded in appreciation and hurried into the castle. Curiously, he encountered people stationed at random points, all similarly dressed and all doing very little. He wondered if they were waiting for a signal and if they had been allocated various look-out positions to warn someone of his arrival and then capture him. Feeling a little paranoid, he made his way towards a group of people in a large empty room, empty except for paintings that adorned all four walls. This was the Long Gallery.

A woman addressing the group was speaking about the largest painting that took pride of place on the gable wall. It was at least six feet tall and surrounded by the thickest gold frame you had ever seen. Those listening were carrying stools, easels and paint-boxes, eager to soak up the atmosphere of the gallery and recreate the masterpiece before them. "This is the infamous portrait of the Sheriff of Nottingham," she announced. "An excellent interpretation in oil. He was said to have a rather sardonic sense of humour and I think this portrays him well. He appears to be smirking at you from whatever angle you look at him." The artists stepped to the right and to the left, testing out the theory.

With a look of contempt, the man glanced at the portrait and at the artists, who appeared in awe of his overrated state of grandeur. He could not bear to look at the grinning portrait any longe, and made a quick exit into the dining room. The table was set with goblets and horn bowls and large, oval server plates. He could almost taste the succulent fruit, sumptuous venison and the rich full-bodied mead. Surely the artists would be better off painting a bowl of fruit than that despicable man?

He wondered where the silver goblets were, and if the women had retired upstairs to read or sew. He was always popular with the ladies. Taking the grand staircase two steps at a time, he hurried along the corridor in search of the master bedroom. It was deserted, preserved in time and untouched by modern society. The imposing black ebony wooden bed, with its heavy curtained canopy, dominated the room and set his mind racing. He wondered who had slept there since he had, and, owing to the fusty smell, who had perhaps died there too. He looked around the room. Had any of the latest occupants left any clues? The dressing table was bare except for a small pair of gold and pearl cufflinks – hardly of use to him, but he pocketed them nonetheless. He eased the writing desk from the wall, hoping to find a letter that might have fallen behind it, and it was then that he saw it: the tiny door to the secret tunnel. He toyed with the idea of climbing inside, knowing that he was not exactly dressed for crawling and that he must attend the court. Suddenly, he heard footsteps and voices along the corridor and within moments the decision was made for him. He clambered inside the tunnel, closing the door behind him. Before daring to move, he tuned in to the conversation that was now taking place in the bedroom.

"And this, ladies and gentleman, is the master bedroom, thought to be where Richard the Lionheart slept, and, while he was away on his Crusades, his brother John also favoured this room. It has very special features most useful for a king, namely its secret tunnel!"

The guide moved his tour group closer to the door and continued to enthral them with his historical tales of gruesome murders and heroic acts of espionage. " And it was from this very tunnel, ladies and gentlemen, that King Edward sprang out, grabbed Mortimer from that bed there, which he was sharing with his lover, Queen

Isabella, and had him executed. Legend has it that her screams can be heard in this room at night, pleading for her lover's life, and that the King's footsteps can often be heard in the tunnel." The excited group lunged forward as the guide reached down and opened the secret door.

From his crouched position some fifty yards or so into the tunnel, he could see the faces of the group peering through the door. He dared not move or breathe until they had closed the door, and then he clambered his way deeper into the narrow sandstone tunnel. Finally, he reached a glint of light arising from a wooden door. Beyond the door he could hear voices, and was certain that he had reached the inn. He had visited the inn on many previous occasions, and wondered if the tunnel would open into the familiar room where he had planned and plotted many of his previous 'crimes'. The inn had afforded him anonymity in the past, and there, in the dark mahogany-boarded room, he had been able to talk freely with his associates without fear of being disturbed. Carefully, he pushed the tunnel door open and saw the legs of two men leaving the room. He emerged from under the table and saw the men heading down some steps towards the exit. They were talking rather loudly, using animated gestures, and seemed to be excited about some imminent event. "I can't wait for later," one exclaimed as he pushed the door open to the small courtyard.

He saw that it was the couple from earlier, the ones he had literally bumped into on the canal towpath. The shorter man withdrew a packet of cigarettes from his breast pocket, offered one to his companion and then lit them both. He could not help but stare at them. He not seen anything like this and wondered what it was that was causing smoke to emit from their mouths and nostrils. Surely they might ignite at any moment and the whole place might go up in flames?

Glancing around the room quickly, he saw that the men had left some drinks on the table and a few belongings. There was something shiny and black with a circular button. It was wafer-thin and half of it was glass and half of it metal. There appeared to be a picture of an apple on the back that had been bitten into. Suddenly it started to vibrate in his hand, which made him drop it abruptly onto the table. He eyed it with mistrust, wondering why coloured flights were now flashing from it and what on earth it could signify. Was this a device to alert people of his presence? Was he being tracked?

The ale looked tempting, and within a minute he had consumed the remaining liquor in both glasses. It tasted rather sweet and gassy but at least it had quenched his thirst for now. Leaving the empty glasses and strange vibrating object, he entered a very busy room where many people were eating. Everyone seemed in deep conversation and once again there was much talk about some forthcoming event. He was beginning to feel paranoid and wondered if these people had come to the city today to watch his trial.

"We'll be heading over straight after we have seen the castle," said one lady to her friend, "so that we can get to our seats and avoid the queues."

Two other ladies had just finished their meals and were making for the exit door in front of him. One reached into her purse and placed two golden-coloured coins and one silver coin on the table they had vacated. It seemed odd to him that someone would deliberately leave money on a table for someone else to find. He stopped to gaze at the dusty, ghostly galleon now encased in glass. According to the plaque nearby, those who had attempted to clean it met a gruesome untimely death. He thought better of it. Perhaps was not a good day to try and clean it. As he squeezed between the diners, some turned away and one remarked aloud about a nearby "unpleasant smell". Passing the recently vacated table, he looked at the coins and considered it his duty to pick them up.

Outside the inn, crowds had gathered to soak up the afternoon sunshine and enjoy a little alfresco dining. He could see the two gentlemen still in the courtyard. They no longer had smoke arising from their mouths, but now he noticed several other people were doing the same thing. In fact, the more he thought about it, the more people he noticed to be doing it. As he stood alone, wondering whether or not to head over to the courtroom early, he took a moment to take in his surroundings. ' Ye Olde Trip To Jerusalem' was painted in old English script on the gable end of the inn. There were no horses tethered to the wall. The only ones he had seen were being deployed as mounts for the increasing presence of police officers.

How things had changed! He had not been to the city in years, but had still expected the people to be friendly. Instead, he found them to be quite hostile, very few making eye contact and even fewer offering conversation. He felt dirty, and repulsive, like an unwelcomed disease. Was he the unpleasant smell that the woman had referred to? Across the street he saw a beggar, sitting cross-legged on a blanket with his dog. Picking up some leftover steak from one of the plates on a nearby table, he made his way over to them. A women wearing several gold bracelets tutted her disapproval and turned towards her companions with a display of disgust. Perhaps she wanted the leftover meal, he thought to himself, but surely a noble woman like her would not have a need for scraps? She had a handbag emblazed with the words 'Louis Vuitton' and he guessed she might have been part of the French aristocracy.

The little dog devoured the treat from the stranger and was almost as happy as his owner, who was now clutching the coins that had been left behind on the table earlier. The streets were buzzing with crowds. He asked one of the mounted officers what the excitement was all about, and was quite taken back by his sarcastic reply. "Are you oblivious, mate?" said the officer. 'It's always like this on Derby Day. Where have you been hiding for the last few years? It's every time County play Forest. We're expecting at least ten thousand in the city tonight and maybe half that number around the bars later!"

Relieved that the crowds had not come to witness his trial, he continued on his way to the courts. He imagined what it must be like to have all those people crammed into the public inns, and, more specifically, who were County and Forest and what exactly were they playing? He guessed it might involve some kind of amphitheatre where slaves or paupers were expected to fight with wild dogs and bulls whilst the richer men placed bets on the last one to be killed. He had never liked such bloodthirsty sports. He passed a group of men on the corner who seemed to running some secret, covert operation from beneath an overcoat. They were selling tickets at overrated prices, but still people were paying for them, eager to get in on the action.

The time was approximately 1.30pm. He knew this because he had recently heard a large bell chime; it seemed to shake the whole city and make everyone look to the skies. "That's the Council House bell!" said a passer-by to his friend. There would be plenty of time before his hearing to go and find it, but, to be honest, he had seen enough of the city and just wanted to get on with proceedings.

Outside the courts the press were gathering in small groups, adjusting their cameras and hoping to catch a glimpse of the accused and their entourages as they entered the court. He saw the security guard that he had met earlier and tried to evade recognition. No such luck!

"Hey there!" called Frank. "I see you found it OK. They're going in now," he added, ushering him towards the assembled reporters.

"Some journalist you are!" added Will, "Not even a notepad, let alone a camera!"

"It's all in my head," replied the stranger. "I make mental notes and write them down later." With that, the two guards shrugged their shoulders and led the way to the press gallery. Without a word, the stranger obligingly followed and found a seat in the back row. He still could not recall who the guard reminded him of, and he turned to his left to sneak another glance. At over six feet tall and much larger than the average gentleman, he was not hard to miss; but his attention was soon drawn to a rather dishevelled-looking man in the dock. He was painfully thin with long, greasy hair and a grey, sunken pallor.

Courtroom 1 was closing the defence hearing of the first case of the day, prior to the much-awaited sentencing of the second case. Although the stranger was unaccustomed to court dealings of this nature, he had worked out that he would also need to be standing in the 'box', as this appeared to be the central focus of proceedings. The accused man looked dazed and withdrawn, and fidgeted constantly with the hem of his clothing. Everyone listened intently as the defence outlined their case.

"This is a man who has been down on his luck for most of his life. He has been raised in poverty and his father was a violent man, often beating him for no apparent reason. He was constantly in trouble for frequent absenteeism from school. Rather than study, he would trawl the streets and back alleys for food. Not surprisingly, he left with no qualifications and found it impossible to seek employment. He quickly became mixed up with 'the wrong kind of people', who took pleasure from inflicting fear in others. With the gang as his newly adopted family, he felt safe and protected. They ran a protection racket and this afforded them money to survive. Like the gang, he soon became addicted to heroin. He was compelled to commit the horrific crimes that he did because he was victim to an evil far beyond his control or the comprehension of this court. He was powerless to resist, and on the day that he broke into the house and seriously battered a woman and her child to within an inch of their lives he was simply following his craving. He needed money to feed his habit and this was an opportunist crime. Heroin had become the Lord and he was the dutiful servant. Voices in his head were telling him to do this. In a vain attempt to destroy the evidence, he set fire to the property. He had no idea that two other children were asleep upstairs in their beds. When he reached home he felt regret immediately, and to his credit it was my client that called the emergency services. Ladies and gentlemen of the jury, I ask you to take this into consideration when making your verdict."

The defendant said nothing, but his defence lawyer continued to address Courtroom 1 with reasons as to why his client should be treated leniently. The press were hurriedly scribbling notes and recording as much information as they could – all hoping to write the best headlines, get the best stories and, as a consequence, sell the most newspapers.

"My client," he continued, "is not an evil man, but a sad product of the society we live in. He has continued to try and survive in absolute poverty and deprivation whilst surrounded by the unfairness of affluence and prosperity. He needs help, not prison, my Lord."

Several people were nodding in agreement and some members of the jury appeared moved to tears. A couple of people shouted, "Here, here !" whilst others clapped. Members of the victim's family called out in disgust, and the press revelled in the circus.

The judge quickly silenced them and resumed an air of authority in the courtroom. He thanked the barrister for his summary and then proceeded to make his own closing speech. He addressed the members of the jury and asked them to deliberate all aspects and circumstances of the crime before retiring to consider their verdict.

As everyone stood and shuffled out of the court, the stranger saw this as his opportunity to adopt his position, ready for his case. He leaped over rows of benches and, with an agility that defied his years, made his way into the box. Courtroom ushers had been busy trying to locate him for the last twenty minutes and were perplexed to now find him standing in the dock as though he had appeared from nowhere. Frank and Will were equally flummoxed, and knew they were in serious trouble if the man disclosed their stupidity. "He's no journalist," exclaimed Frank. "This is the main man!"

"How did you get here?" asked the usher.

Frank and Will sloped down the wall against which they were leaning, hoping not to be exposed by the stranger. "It's a long story,' he replied, glancing over at the guards. "But I'm here now and ready to proceed."

"Do you not have a representative?" asked the puzzled usher, pretty sure there were no lawyers he had missed in the foyer. "No, sir," he replied. "Ought I require one?" There was no time to await a reply.

"Can the defendant please stand," called the judge, who then proceeded to shock the court with the following statement. "This jury has deliberated long and hard in your absence and today is finally able to return a verdict in relation to your alleged crimes. You may have enjoyed years of acclaimed status, but the truth is far from heroic. You are accused of anti-clericalism, seeking to remove the church and all that it entails from the lives of honest people. You show a lack of respect towards authority and your continual animosity towards our sheriff is most apparent. You have no respect for our monarch and continue to incite rebellion, spreading your treason and treacherous thoughts like poison."

A sharp intake of breath echoed around the courtroom as people could not believe their ears. Heads turned from left to right, looking for a reaction from the accused and then back to the judge. You could have heard a pin drop.

"You pay no taxes and think that you are exempt whilst others manage to pay. You continuously take it upon yourself to steal from others and in the year 1217 alone ambushed no less than thirty-four gentlemen – distinguished gentlemen, might I add."

The judge continued, "You are a tyrant, an outlaw, and out of control. Indeed, you are nothing more than a nomadic felon who is quite simply a danger to society. You have no representative to speak on your behalf and so, Robin Hood, I therefore sentence you to life imprisonment. You will be taken to the cells, from where you will be moved imminently to a maximum security jail. There you will remain until you die. Take him down."

Gasps of abhorrence echoed from the public gallery, and the stranger felt that the eyes of a hundred people were boring a hole in his soul. Where were his comrades when he needed them? What had happened to solidarity and common sense? If only he had his bow and arrows with him, he could take the lot of them out in a few minutes. Still, he had come to accept his fate and that he would do with dignity. On no account would he show fear of or subordination to authority.

The two security guards stepped forward and rather aggressively, perhaps in a show of respect to the court, grabbed Robin and marched him down the steps to the cells below. A metal door was unlocked and he was thrust inside with a sandwich and a Styrofoam cup of coffee. The cell was bare except for a stainless steel toilet, a naked light bulb and a built-in concrete bed that at least had a thin foam mattress. The door slammed closed behind him and he found himself alone. It had all been a waste of time, his plea to return and clear his name. His crimes appeared more heinous now to the people of Nottingham than they did in the thirteenth century. He thought about the newspaper he had seen earlier, and how men were still at war with each other over the same things despite the passing of over seven hundred years.

Men still lust after the wives of others and do not stay true to their vows. They still over-indulge with food and drink, often wasting it while others have to starve. Some have a desperate need to acquire possessions, often superfluous to requirement in a way of enriching their power or status. Others see this, and in turn they want more than they have got and seek ways to acquire it. Some men display an inordinate self-esteem and air of supremacy, causing others to bring about their downfall. Men who actually choose to be idle infuriate those that are working hard, and this whole 'melting pot' can 'boil over', producing extreme anger at any time. In essence, nothing has changed. These are the seven deadly sins: lust, gluttony, greed, envy, pride, sloth and wrath. They are still as evident today as they were hundreds of years ago.

He thought about the young man in the dock before him and wondered if the jury would consider his circumstances, or if his fate would be similar to his. He thought about the things he had seen and wondered if he would ever get to sample what a cigarette tasted like, and what the attraction to drugs was all about. His only vice had been ale. Feeling rather hungry, he turned his attention to the triangular cardboard box he had been given. 'Tuna mayonnaise' it read on the front and, not having a clue what he was eating, he scoffed it ravenously, washed it down with his coffee and enjoyed them both immensely.

The cell was becoming quite cold, and he wondered where the street beggar and his dog were sleeping tonight and if they had shelter. He tucked his trousers deeper into his boots to keep in the warmth and it was then that he felt his dagger. With nothing else to do, he pulled it from his boot and began etching his mark into the white plastered walls. When he was satisfied that his work was complete, he dropped the dagger to the floor and drifted into restless sleep.

The morning came slowly and at approximately 6am the door was sharply pushed open. The light had remained on all night, and Robin was still very tired. In walked Frank, his belly almost a second before him, and in an instant Robin recalled where he had seen him before. He leapt from the bed with elation. "Friar Tuck!" he exclaimed 'And my dear friend, Will Scarlet. How did I not recognise you?"

Frank embraced his comrade and, when looking over his shoulder was mortified to see the jewelled dagger on the cell floor. "We are equally to blame for not recognising you, our dear friend," he said. "Listen, Robin. We would have lost our jobs if it were not for you keeping quiet yesterday. We let you into the court thinking you were a reporter, and the fact that you were armed would have most certainly resulted in our P45s."

"P45s?" said Robin, confused.

"Look, there's no time to waste," said Frank. "We are escorting you to Manchester prison now and the van is outside waiting. Change into these clothes and we will return in two minutes."

Will smiled, gave a nod of his head and reached in his pocket for the van keys. "I had a feeling it was you. I never actually got to thank you for saving my wife from her loveless marriage back then," he said, and left with a wink.

The clothes seemed rather comfortable and Robin felt warm and clean. He particularly liked the soft, pliable shoes with a large, black tick emblem on the side. They made his feet feel free and he was sure that they would be great for climbing. Will and Frank returned, gathered the discarded clothes into a bag and, of course, the dagger. Will ushered Robin outside, while Frank lingered a few moments and thrust the dagger into the lock, forcibly damaging the internal locking mechanism. He carefully pulled the cell door closed, but failed to notice Robin's handiwork on the wall.

There wasn't a soul in sight, so he could not judge the reactions of others, but Robin thought that his previous attire was perhaps the reason why people had been staring at him or snubbing him. His long, flapping coat with plenty of 'swoosh" was perhaps not the height of fashion any more. The city was still sleeping, following the excitement of last night's football match. Forest had apparently won. Once outside, he was bundled into an old transit van, while his companions sat in the front. It smelt fusty and he noticed a few maggots squirming on the floor. It looked as though a partition had been made separating the rear from the cab, and this prevented him from attempting any form of communication. They were not acting like his good friends now.

Robin could see out of the rear windows and was not sad to leave the city behind. It had changed so much and there were things with coloured lights that seemed to be everywhere, causing the traffic to stop and start. It seemed like an eternity before they were heading out into the countryside. Robin could see large green signs by the roadside and the symbols A614 seemed to appear again and again. Perhaps it was a code name for a secret place. He looked around the van, thinking what he could use to escape and, other than a couple of old fishing rods and a battered wicker basket there was little that inspired him.

Within approximately twenty minutes the van turned left and made its way down a narrow dirt track before came to a standstill. He heard the front doors open and close and then saw the men standing behind the vehicle. The brightness of the morning sun flooded into the van, as the rear doors were swung open.

"Go !" said Frank. "Run, and make a new life for yourself. This is the least we can do for you!"

Robin was overwhelmed. He had misjudged their intentions. Before him he saw a kaleidoscope of Nature's colours against the clear blue sky: the emeralds, olives, khakis, limes and greens; the russets, tans, auburns, coffees and browns – the beautiful spectacle that was unforgettably Sherwood Forest. He inhaled deeply, taking in the welcoming aromas of the evergreens and the flourishing wild garlic. He had come home. With tear-soaked eyes, he hugged his friends for the final time, and then ran into the embrace of the forest. Frank and Will watched until he disappeared out of sight.

It all seemed surreal. The two men drove in silence. There was little to say. Now and again they looked at the bag of clothing in the foot-well and, as if both thinking the same thing, they agreed to stop once more and dispose of the 'evidence'. Will pulled up alongside the River Maun near Ollerton. They emptied the contents of the bag onto the riverbank, turned out the pockets and selected one or two souvenirs between them. The unwanted items were bundled back into the bag, along with some stones, before Frank hurled it into the river. Thankfully neither of them was at work that weekend and they had agreed to meet up on Sunday for a day of fishing.

That day could not come soon enough. All weekend the two

friends had questioned their sanity and replayed the events of that Friday over and over in their heads. Sitting in their garden chairs by the lake at Bevercotes, rods in hand, Frank finally broke the peace. "Do you really think it was him, Will? Did we really meet him again?"

Suddenly, Frank's rod started to bend and his attention was distracted away from the conversation. It was the first bite of the day, so he did not want to miss it. He stood up excitedly and began reeling his catch in. Will threw down his newspaper and assisted by holding out the landing net. A large eel emerged from the water, wriggling violently on the hook. It was every fisherman's nightmare. They often swallowed the hook whole, meaning the line had to be disgorged from the depths of their guts or the creatures had to be simply killed and put out of their misery. If only the damn thing would keep still so a decision could be made. Frank, however, knew a trick. He had learned from his father that if you took a sheaf knife and carved a cross in the soft ground, and laid the eel in it, it would lie perfectly still and allow the hook to be removed. He reached into his fishing basket and pulled out a rather ostentatious- looking gold dagger with a row of beautiful green emeralds set into the quillion. With it, he scored a cross on the grassy bank and in it he placed the eel. True to word, it kept perfectly still, enabling Will to remove the hook from the depths of its belly. Will tossed the creature back into the lake while Frank re-baited the hook with some rather juicy maggots.

Will returned his attention to his newspaper. It had fallen open on the second page and he could not quite believe his eyes. In large letters it read: 'Notorious Outlaw Escapes From Cell Before Transfer To Prison'. He reached from his chair, picked up the newspaper and hitched up his jumper sleeves as though meaning business. A delicate pearl cufflink caught the sunlight and glinted at Frank. This made Frank smile, and look admiringly down at his own feet. He loved his newly acquired, rather unfashionable boots with pointed toes. Not quite suitable for fishing but fabulous noneth less. "What does it say, Will?" asked Frank, eager to know more.

Will read aloud from the paper: 'The long-awaited verdict from the Robin Hood Trial was delivered in Courtroom 1 of Nottingham Crown Court on Friday. Robin Hood of Loxley was found guilty of his accused crimes, perhaps the worse that Nottingham has ever encountered, and was sentenced to life imprisonment. He showed no remorse, in fact no emotion, as he was escorted down to the cells. The next day, when prison officials came to escort him to the category A prison in Manchester, they found the cell to be empty. He had broken the lock with a sharp, pointed instrument and made his escape. There, on the cell wall, he had scrolled the following words:

'And when they seek
to oppress you
And when they try
to destroy you,
Rise and rise again
Like the Phoenix
from the ashes
Until the lambs
have become lions
and the rule of Darkness
is no more.'

The general public have been warned not to approach him as he is potentially very dangerous.'

"Well, I think that answers our question!!" said Frank, opening two cans of beer from his chiller bag and passing one over to Will.

"Indeed, it does," replied Will with a huge grin, offering his can out to clink with Frank's. "Cheers, my friend. Indeed it does!"

CHRISTOPHER GOLDSMITH

A WINDMILL'S TALE

Usually I write poems, but have always loved stories. So this was an opportunity to write something in a new genre and try something different from poems and performance poetry, which has taken up much of my life over the last thirty years or so.

Having lived in Retford since 1984, I've always been aware of the windmill at Leverton and it seemed such an iconic part of the landscape that I wanted to include it.

Also, I didn't want to have a ghost story and don't really know enough about Robin Hood and the like to make it credible. I did take liberties with the geography of the park – that was inspired by the park I used to play in as a kid, Walmer Bridge Rec. The four lads are all based on my friends who I spent so much time with all those years ago, and (trivia fans) there is an element of Slade there, too, in their names. I'll leave you to work that one out.

It was great fun writing the story, but I wish I'd started it earlier. Inevitably, there's things I'd change, edit, develop – but isn't that always the case.

Lastly, why Christopher Goldsmith and not Paul Cookson? I wanted to make it completely separate from Paul Cookson the poet. However, I did find out that Christopher Goldsmith was my original name before I was adopted at birth – so it's separate, but the same as well.

A WINDMILL'S TALE

Who cares that North Leverton with Habblesthorpe is the longest place name in England?

Nev didn't.

Neither did Lee. Or Dave. Or Donno for that matter.

They cared about the windmill, though. Especially as it made them famous. Briefly. And even 'briefly' is a long time – especially in North Leverton with Habblesthorpe.

Long, long ago, in a galaxy far away, as a famous story once started… It was a different time, a different world, where summers seemed longer, the sun shone brighter, days were carefree, bikes were a passport to freedom and computers were only seen in Star Trek.

School was out for the summer. In the case of Nev, Lee, Dave and Donno, school was out for ever. At least Primary School was. It was a summer of freedom where the old was left behind and the new was two months away. So naturally they didn't think about it. Days were filled with bike rides, kick-abouts, rope swings and camping out in Old Man Chandler's field. Old Man Chandler didn't mind. He knew Nev's granddad, so that was that.

As long as they could remember and as long as they'd had bikes, the windmill had always been important. They'd ridden past it a million times, but still it looked impressive against the Nottinghamshire sky.

It was a centurion, a pirate galleon, an alien spaceship, a giant's helmet, a castle where Robin Hood once hid, a haunted house, a time machine and a thousand other things. But it had never been this.

It was Nev's idea – but all Donno's fault after an unfortunate incident with Mad Cow Turton, the monster dinner lady, just before Easter.

Technically speaking, he didn't start the food fight. That was Gibbon Boy, although Donno had left a banana on his plate and started the laughter and the chest-beating when Wayne Taylor had returned to his seat.

Wayne Taylor (or Gibbon Boy as everyone knew him) was a little boy with big friends. A snivelling little baby worm. Literally. With a nose that was always running, he constantly had to wipe away the drips with one of the many personalised hankies his overbearing mother made him carry round. He didn't like it if anyone mentioned the hankies with his initials in the corner – especially as his middle name was Edwin. So his hankies were wet by nature and W.E.T by name. Not big or brave enough to bully anyone by himself, he was the bully's hanger-on, the one who joined in just after they had started their dark magic. Under their spell he'd do their bidding and take their punishment, running errands like a scurrying monkey – hence the name.

Nev, Lee, Dave and Donno weren't the cool kids, neither were they the bullied. They were the invisible ones in the middle.

But Gibbon Boy had it coming. Big style. All that week he'd been showing off, and that Wednesday morning had got Donno in trouble with Mr D (Big D). Big D was okay as a teacher, often funny, but you didn't want to get on his bad side. Which was huge – as was he. Over six feet tall and nearly as wide, his school chair hardly seemed strong enough for his height, width and weight, and it creaked ominously every time he lowered that gargantuan frame down. Because Donno had laughed quickest and loudest at the inevitable when the chair legs splayed and the wood splintered,

Big D naturally assumed he was guilty and somehow compliant in the events. That had been Gibbon Boy and his father's hacksaw before school started.

If a teacher falls off a chair in front of their class it's always funny. If a mountain-sized teacher does so and their trousers rip in the process – bingo! So, as the laughter died down and Big D got up, it was Donno who snorted the last guffaw. First to laugh and last to stop equalled guilt with Big D, so not only was Donno subjected to a verbal volcano, but he was relieved of his free time for the rest of the week. And Big D spent the rest of the day in tracksuit bottoms that were too tight and most unsightly.

Hence the banana. Then the flying fish finger … and, as one thing led to another, the massive dollop of chocolate sponge and custard that flew from the serving spoon and would have hit Gibbon Boy on the head … if only Mad Cow Turton hadn't got in the way. With her nose. She was bending over, trying to stop Gibbon Boy from hurling the contents of his pudding bowl in the direction of Donno, Nev, Lee and Dave when …

It was a moment they all remembered. A moment everyone remembered. The sort of moment you never forget and always happens in slow motion: the gentle arc of the chocolate sponge, the gloopy comet custard trail and the inevitable but perfect SPLAT! as it hit her full on the nose and spread across that angry purple face.

Woooooaaaah … silence. The silence before the storm.

But it was worth it. Donno lost another week of playtimes and had a letter for his parents in his hand by home-time.

"That's it. I've had enough. S'not fair," he grumbled as the four of them rode their bikes home that night.

He was still moaning as they reached the park. Going on and on about revenge and how he'd get Mad Cow Turton. And Gibbon Boy. And Big D. And anyone else for that matter.

They'd always met at the park ever since they were in the Infants. Safe and nearby, it was the first place parents let their kids out unsupervised. It was surrounded on three sides by houses, so there was always some nosey parker supervising something. But when you were young you thought you were free.

Their best waking hours had been spent there. Well, there and the windmill. It was where they played football, tig, hide and seek, soldiers ... everything. Where they planned adventures. Where friendships start.

Nev burped. He was good at burping. No, that was a lie. He was great at burping. He could burp the alphabet and say words of four syllables with one burp. He'd once made Julie West feel sick with the ferocity of his belches.

Dave was showing off as usual, swinging the highest he could on the swing. Always trying to be the centre of attention. Which was strange really – considering his mum cut his hair. Well, not so much cut, as attacked his hair. With what looked like crimping scissors on the fringe. He didn't care that his hair seemed to stick out in a hundred different directions – he loved the attention.

Lee ... wel,l he was the quiet one. Clever. Didn't say much but when he did it was worth listening. He didn't come across as the leader but in many ways he was.

And Donno? Donno was Donno ... always in trouble, always the fall guy – anything for a laugh.

Nev burped again, and pretended to waft the bad breath into Lee's face.

"Give it a rest! What did you have for dinner? Your mum's socks and your dad's pants?" said Lee.

"Naah – that's me tea," chuckled Nev and burped again.

BADOING! THWACK! BADOING! THWACK! BADOING! THWACK!

Donno was kicking his football against a fence. Not just any fence, though.

“Are you mad?” shouted Nev.

“You’ll get us all done now!” echoed Dave.

“Pratt.” Lee.

“That fence is her big fat backside,” laughed Donno.

BADOING! THWACK!

Mad Cow Turton’s house backed on to the park. It was her fence that was being used as a wall for Donno’s football. Her fence was perfect, in that the fence poles were just the right distance apart for a set of goals. Perfect for that – but not perfect when shots flew over the ‘crossbar’. The Garden Of The Lost – they never came back. Three caseballs, two plastic floaters, four tennis balls, one cricket ball and, on one occasion, a boomerang that didn’t work.

BADOING! THWACK! BADOING! THWACK! BADOING

They turned and looked at Donno. Donno looked back and shrugged his shoulders. “What?”

“You’ll never get that back now. You know what she’s like,” said Dave, shaking his head.

“Great shot, Pele. Three points to Wigan!” called Nev.

“Pratt.” Lee.

“That’s what you think. I’ll get it now. Right now.”

And before they could argue, Donno was over the fence. The ball arced back and, shortly after, so did Donno.

“BIKES! NOW!”

Five minutes later, sweating, breathless and laughing, they sat in the shade of the windmill.

"Blimey, that was close. Idiot!" said Lee.

"Did she see you?" asked Dave.

"'Ey up! Have you put on weight?" queried Nev, pointing at the bulge under Donno's school jumper.

Donno stood up, put his hand up his jumper and, with the dramatic flourish of a TV magician, held up the biggest pair of bloomers they had ever seen. Red, flannelette, elasticated, with a frilly bit round the knees.

"Ta-daaah!"

"No ..."

"You haven't ...?"

"They can't be ..."

But they were. Mad Cow Turton's big, red bloomers.

"I hope they're clean," said Nev, pulling a face and wrinkling his nose.

"Why? Just ... why?" said Lee.

"Dunno. They were just ... there," said Donno, shrugging his shoulders and smiling.

"Put 'em on, then!" laughed Dave.

In fact, they were so big that Dave could stand in one leg and Donno in the other. Tweedledee and Tweedledum in bloomers. Together they pretended to be her:

"Sit down!"

"Eat your cabbage!"

"Don't move until you are told."

"You, boy! Office – now!"

And they wobbled round, bottoms sticking out, while Nev and Lee just laughed fit to burst, tears streaming down their faces.

"That's all very funny," said Lee eventually, "but what you gonna do with 'em now?"

"Dunno," said Donno.

But ten minutes later they had a plan. And what a plan …

Nev had been lying down looking at the sails of the windmill against the blue sky when he started giggling. This turned into a full-scale laughing fit. Approval was instantaneous. Agreement, total.

And so it was that, there and then, as the sun shone above the windmill and Donno and Dave still parading like Siamese twins in bloomers, they decided that the sails would become the biggest washing line that North Leverton with Habblesthorpe had ever seen.

A week later they had a plan. Two weeks later that plan was starting to take shape.

In addition to the big, red bloomers of Mad Cow Turton, they'd found Big D's ripped trousers in a storeroom from that fateful day after he'd changed into a spare pare of tracksuit bottoms. Talking of tracksuits, they'd managed to appropriate the tracky top of PE teacher, Mr Chambers – the one with Champ Chambers on the back.

As well as …

Reverend Walkley's cassock – left hung up in the staffroom after the final assembly, while everyone had snacks in the hall.

One school flag – last used in 1945 and found on top of a cupboard in Class 5.

The backdrop from the school play from five years ago, painted and embroidered by the infants and showed a variety of animals entering Noah's Ark. These ranged from lions, tigers, turtles, spiders (as big as the lions), kangaroos and at least four pterodactyls, a brontosaurus and an alien.

A Jolly Roger from Year 3's pirate assembly.

Mrs Morrison's Nottingham Forest Scarf.

And the biggest pair of Y-fronts ever seen. Strictly speaking they weren't actually underpants. They were originally the grubbiest old sheet that had covered Old Man Chandler's Massey Ferguson tractor, but with a bit of creative cutting with rusty garden shears and left-over creosote they were indeed the biggest pair of Y-fronts ever. It was Donno's idea to write Big D on them. No prizes for guessing where.

These acquisitions didn't all happen at once: that was the clever part. A bit at a time, here and there, most went unnoticed. There was no crime wave at school, nothing overtly suspicious – apart from the bulging bin bag under Lee's bed. But his mum and dad never dared to look there, so that was no problem.

Camping out in moth-eaten tents was something most kids did at some time in the summer holidays. Even Gibbon Boy and his cronies had tents, but Nev and the boys never camped out in the same fields or at the same time if they could help it.

Old Man Chandler had several fields and after haymaking had been completed didn't mind the lads pitching up. They chose one far away from the road and put up their battered four-man tent in a corner behind a hedge and in the shade of a tree. You'd have to go in the actual field looking for them to find them – and nobody did.

Once the tent was up it took an afternoon of bike rides to get everything they needed in there: sleeping bags, torches, plastic plates, portable stove, frying pan, bacon, bread … four bottles of fizzy pop, a multipack of crisps and chocolate bars and sweets too numerous to mention. Oh – and the bulging bin bag from beneath Lee's bed. And a washing line and pegs bought from Wilko's in town weeks before.

It was never a hassle trying to persuade parents about camping out. Sometimes there'd be weeks where they almost lived in that tent, just going home or to each other's for meals and toilet stops.

"Aaaah .... the freedom ... the sweet relief," breathed Nev.

"You can't beat an outdoor wee," Dave agreed.

"I can," laughed Donno, as he arched his back and sprayed upwards.

"Puerile." Lee.

"Poo-rile, more like," quipped Donno and then, as if to prove his point, cocked one leg and farted. Loudly.

Flatulence was a badge of honour. Volume, variety of sound and pungency were always important and sought-after but, to be honest, any act of flatulence was funny. Competitive too. Donno was currently the champion. To be fair, he was always the champion.

As the sun went down, the four lay outside their tent looking up and smiling.

"Tonight's the night then, boys," chuckled Nev.

"Indeed it is, indeed it is," grinned Lee.

Not everything would go exactly to plan; things never did, but they'd been through it time and again over the weeks and months. Every time they'd ridden past the windmill they'd stopped and looked, picturing their daring and going through every detail.

It would be after midnight. They wouldn't use torches unless they had to. They'd wear black jumpers and hats. Dave had suggested black gloves too – just in case of fingerprints. That motion wasn't carried, although it did give the others welcome ammunition for the somewhat inevitable and merciless mickey- taking.

No – the biggest problem by far was how they were going to get the washing line actually onto the sails. Especially as the sails were at least twenty feet off the ground. Lee had solved that one, eventually.

"What time is it?" asked Dave from his sleeping bag.

"Half nine," answered Lee.

"Ages yet," said Nev.

Donno proved his champion status. Laughter, mock disgust, theatrical holding of the nose, pretend choking, coughing, spluttering and dramatic wafting of air took them all the way up to cowboy time.

"Why's it called 'cowboy time', then?" said Dave, quizzically.

As one voice the three-part disharmony that was the theme from The Lone Ranger: "Tentotentotentotentotentoten! Tentotentotentotentoteeeeennnnnn!"

"Aaah, the old ones are the best!" laughed Nev.

And indeed they were. The next two hours were spent telling old jokes they'd heard a million times before, demolishing the sweets and crisps, burping words and laughing. Just laughing. That's what friends did. Made each other laugh, laughed at each other, laughed at everyone else. As often as possible. There'd be a silence, then one of them would say something, usually a phrase that brought back immediate memories or a nickname. Or a rude word in a silly voice. Always a winner.

Then there were the ghost stories about the legend of 'Hairy Face' in Old Man Chandler's big shed. No one had ever seen 'Hairy Face'; they couldn't even remember who'd started the stories, but all creakings and shadows became his and the legend grew – to the point where they almost believed there actually was a yeti-like, werewolf type of beast.

They took it in turns to tell 'Hairy Face' stories. Nev was always the best at making up grisly and gruesome stories and tonight was no exception: Hairy Face and The Hanging Man. He even told it with the torch under his chin.

" … and the last thing old Farmer Wignall saw was Hairy Face as the noose tightened around his neck. Hairy Face breathed deathly fumes into the face of the frightened farmer and then kicked the potato boxes from beneath him with a clawed foot. And he dangled from the rafters in his own shed. For days. And days. And days. Until the worms had eaten his eyes …"

"Stop. What was that?" hissed Dave.

"What was what?" said Lee.

"That noise."

"What noise?"

"That noise outside."

"What noise outside?"

"I didn't hear a noise."

"I did."

"Well, you go and look, then."

"I'm not looking."

"Chicken."

"It was just the wind."

"No … this was just the wind," said Donno. "Noooooooooooo!"

Five minutes later they were all out of the tent in the cold night air. Jumpers, hats and coats on.

"'Ey, Dave, have these!" Nev tossed him a pair of his gran's pink leather gloves. "Don't want to leave fingerprints, do we, Sherlock?"

"Ha-de- ha – very witty! Are they yours, you big girl?" Dave threw them back.

"Come on, ladies, we got stuff to do," sighed Lee as he heaved the bin bag out of the tent.

"That's gonna bust open," said Donno.

"I know, I know. That's why I'm putting it in my sleeping bag and we'll carry it that way."

"Like the dead body in Nev's story."

It was a fifteen-minute walk to the windmill from Old Man Chandler's field. They'd done this before. Midnight rambles, seeing who could frighten the others most, seeing who jumped the furthest. Tonight there was none of that. No joking now.

Dave zipped the tent up. Even that sounded loud in the stillness of the night. A gentle breeze ruffled the leaves above their heads and branches creaked softly. They all shivered in the moonlight as a distant owl hooted.

"Right, let's go. Let's do it," whispered Lee and held out his hand.

The others knew what to do. Four right hands on top of each other as they all faced inwards. "All for one ... and one for all." Four voices breathed these words together. Words they'd normally shout and chant.

"Just like the three musketeers," said Nev.

"But there's four: Dartagnan, Aramis, Porthos and the other one. So why is it called the Three Musketeers?" asked Dave.

"Shut up!"

"Not now, idiot!"

The four musketeers took their first steps across the stubbly grass. Lee and Nev carried the sleeping bag between them. Donno and Dave went slightly ahead: army lookouts, Red Indian scouts, even though they all knew the way. Silence had never seemed so loud. Every squeak of trainer on wet grass sounded like a scream. Donno trod on a stick. They all stopped and looked around. But of course there was no-one around to hear the cracking of the stick. Out of the field and down the track. That was the easy bit. Then they had to go a few hundred yards along the main road out of the village before they got to the lane that led to the windmill.

So far, so good. No cars, no late night dog walkers. They jogged as much as they could on this stretch, and had almost got to the lane when the unmistakable sound of an engine rumbled and headlights shone in the distance.

"Quick! Get to the lane and get behind the hedge," Lee ordered.

Headlights snaked closer. Dave and Donno had made it and were not only behind the hedge but in the ditch as well. The engine roared ever louder as the car was about to turn the final corner. Nev and Lee were desperately trying to run and carry the sleeping bag at the same time. Together. It all happened at once. Nev stumbled; the bag fell; he went to pick it up, only for Lee to kick it away from him into the verge, and, before he knew it, Lee was running, pulling him and they got to the track just as the car turned the corner. A last-gasp dive and they sprawled in the wet grass as the beam lit the spot they had just vacated. The searchlight passed around the corner and over the blue shiny fabric of the sleeping bag. To the four sets of eyes widening in the shadows it seemed like a spotlight, highlighting their secret. Obvious, unmissable and definitely suspicious. But in reality it was a split second and the red lights of the car disappeared around the next corner.

"That was close, Nev."

"Too close, mate, too close."

"Quick – get the sleeping bag."

They'd only just got back to the hedge with Dave and Donno when an engine roared and headlights on full beam turned the corner from the village. Brakes squealed as the car came to a halt. Just by the verge. Just where the bright blue sleeping bag had been. The driver killed the engine. Two doors thunked open. Two figures stepped out, footsteps crunching on the gravel.

"I'm sure I saw something here," a loud and confident voice boomed in the stillness.

The headlights cast pools of light straight ahead, illuminating the grass verge and every single branch and bramble in the hedge, the hedge just above their heads, as the four lads tried not to breathe in the ditch. Every muscle tightened and tensed, they dared not move. Eyes closed, faces down, ears open.

The two men who had got out of the car were still talking.

"Must have been mistaken."

"Looked like a body, though."

"A body! Where?"

"Just here."

And they wandered over to the grass verge.

"No body here. And nobody here, mate."

They were just about to turn and go back to the car when the taller of the two men leant down and picked something up.

"What's that?"

"Hat of some sort"

Four boys froze in the ditch. Nev opened his eyes and silently put a hand to his head. No hat.

"Just a woolly hat."

My hat, thought Nev. Did my mum put my name in it for school?

"Could be anybody's."

"True. Could have been here ages. Doesn't mean anything."

"Come on, mate. Nothing doing here. Let's go."

"I'm just going to have a look over there – by that hedge."

The four musketeers tensed. Footsteps crunched louder. They tensed even more. Louder – and then the swish of wet grass.

The engine growled and headlights flashed on and off as the car slowly moved towards the hedge. The car reversed into the track. A door clunked shut and with a roar the car was gone. Back towards the village.

The four musketeers didn't move a muscle. Apart from Donno.

"Sorry lads, I've been holding that one in for ages."

"Me too," giggled Dave and outshone Donno in every aspect.

"Top trumps – without the cards!" laughed Nev.

"Idiots! I'm surrounded by idiots!" Lee shook his head. "And smelly ones at that!"

Laughter breaks any nervous silence and when wind has broken the silence first, the laughter doubles. And so it did. Lying in a ditch in the cold night air trying to stifle the guffawing, their bodies shook until the laughter turned to a cold shiver.

"Best get my hat," said Nev at last. But he couldn't find it. No-one found it that night. Or ever. At that moment it was in an overcoat pocket of a man in a car on his way to Gainsborough. He later threw it away idly.

"I don't think my mum had sewn my name in it, though." Nev was now carrying one end of the sleeping bag and trying to convince the others that the hat wouldn't be evidence in a crime that they hadn't yet committed.

Lee put his end down and looked up. The windmill, silent, gargantuan and somehow more mysterious against the black sky.

"Are we still doing this?" he asked.

The other three smiled and nodded in the dark. "Right – let's do it and get the hell out of here."

Unzipping the sleeping bag, they laid everything out on the ground, the windmill standing guard over them. Lee got the washing line and unravelled it. It had taken him ages to work out how to suspend the line between the two sails. Each of the sails had a series of wooden slats with gaps between them. But they were at least twenty feet off the ground and how do you reach them and tie knots around the slats? You don't. Well, you have to reach them in some way, obviously.

That was done thanks to several boxes, numerous hay bales, a ladder that didn't reach that far and a long wooden clothes prop that they had hidden in the woodpile round the back some weeks back. It was still there. Lee got the washing line, tied a spanner round one end and tested the weight.

It was difficult working in the dark. They were wet and cold from the ditch, nervous because of the car and the lost hat, but they'd talked about it over and over and knew what to do.

The boxes were old, square and wooden. Solid too. Made to last. Made to carry potatoes, grain, carrots and whatever else farmers needed carrying. But before the boxes – the bales. Most farms had hay this time of year and the fields next to the windmill were no different. All around the field were stacked bales, in sixes or eights, waiting for the tractor and trailer to come and load them and take them away.

Tonight, though, the bales would not be in the field but below the sail of the windmill. It took ages and it was hard getting them over the fence, but eventually eight of them had made a square base. Six more then went on top of them. Then four more. Like a pyramid, with no point. On top of the four, the wooden boxes were placed carefully. On top of the boxes went the step-ladder.

"Are you sure that's safe?" Nev was looking up at it and shaking his head.

"It'd better be." Donno shuddered.

"It'll have to be," said Dave, as he climbed on the first row of bales.

"Not so fast." Lee motioned for Dave to come down. "We've got to do this carefully."

"Yes – and we've got to do it tonight, so gerramoveon!"

Dave climbed the pyramid, clambered onto the boxes and then gingerly started on the ladder, which was now shaking and swaying. Nev handed him the clothes prop. The washing line was entwined all around the prop except for the end. At the top of the prop was the groove, and that's where the washing line end was dangling. Dangling about three feet with the spanner tied on.

Lifting the prop skywards and sail-wards, Dave held his breath and tried to ignore the swaying of the ladder as the weight of the prop unbalanced him. Nev and Donno were leaning over the boxes and holding the ladder at the base, but it still looked as if it could fall at any moment. Lee had the washing line and was letting it out as Dave prodded the prop. It clacked against the sale and the line nearly came out of the groove at the top. Steadying himself, he stretched again, this time with more deliberation and care. The end of the prop found a slat. Now it was a case of getting the line through the gap between the slats. In the dark. Dave's arms stretched and stiffened as he tried to guide the prop gently along the slat and get the weighted line through the slat. He almost did it twice; then the line came out of the groove.

He swore quietly, brought the prop down and balanced the line again. He found he slat again, twisted the prop a little and the end with the spanner fell through. "Yessss!"

"Now untwist the line carefully around the prop and try and feed that through too," said Lee.

"I know. I'm not a complete idiot."

"Why? Which bit's missing?"

"Shut it, Nev! You come and do it if you think you're so clever."

Twisting the prop slowly, the line came away a bit at a time and Dave managed to guide a bit more through. Once he'd untwisted it all from the prop he had the groove under the line, and as Lee fed more out, he pushed it towards the slat until the weight of the spanner did its job. The spanner swung like a pendulum above Dave, who now used the prop to guide the line and spanner downwards. The spanner caught in the groove and there it was, in his hands. "Yesssssss!"

Back on the ground he pulled the spanner and line down and Lee was replacing the spanner with two short planks he'd nailed together the previous week and hidden in the wood pile. He knotted the line several times and tested it in his hands. Seemed firm enough.

"Right, you two, pull the washing line back our way."

Nev and Donno did as they were told and just as they'd planned, and bingo! The line came to a halt as the two short planks criss-crossed and wedged behind the slat. A little tug to make sure everything was okay. It was.

The next stage was pegging the washing on the line: the bloomers, the ripped trousers, the tracksuit top, the cassock, pirate flag, back drop, the football scarf and last, but not least, the biggest pair of Y-fronts in the world.

"Okay, now all we have to do is move the bales and boxes under the other sail and do it all again," said Lee at last.

"That's going to take ages," sighed Donno.

"Thought it was going to be easier than this," breathed Nev.

They'd just moved the ladder and the boxes when a deep voice said, "Okay then you lot?"

Lee, Nev and Donno looked up and stopped dead in their tracks.

"Don't wet your knickers, ladies. It's only little old me!"

Dave was shinning along the arm of the sail. "Give me the line. I can just about reach from here if you give me the prop."

Lee had re-tied the spanner at the other end and was now guiding the prop towards Dave. Nev and Donno tried to take the weight of the washing as best they could while Dave fished one- handed with the prop reaching toward the slat. He got it first time and the spanner clinked through. Then it was a case of guiding the line through gently, as the weight of the spanner wasn't enough against the weight of the washing. Eventually enough line was through to make a grab for it. Lee got it and pulled. Donno and Nev helping as the washing line took shape. Five minutes later, the spanner had been replaced with another two short planks, and gravity had done the rest. True, the washing line bowed a little, but it didn't fall or break and everything hung there in the dark.

They were planning to move the bales and boxes back ... but they didn't. Just left them where they'd finished with them, right under the sail. None of them noticed Donno reach into his pocket and leave something under the boxes before they left the scene.

"So, clever clogs, how did you do that?" asked Lee. They were back in the tent, sweaty, aching but elated and celebrating with fizzy pop and chocolate at three o'clock in the morning.

"Well, the windmill door wasn't locked. I found some stairs and a window and ... well, you know how good I am at climbing and showing off!"

Laughter and conversation dried up as exhaustion took its toll. Sleep and relief. But not for long. The sun rises early in the summer, and so do the birds. Morning sunlight illuminated the orange tent and it seemed God had turned the volume up on the dawn chorus. Especially the rooks and crows.

One by one, the four woke. They stretched, yawned, wiped their eyes and staggered outside.

"Who's got the matches?" grunted Nev. "Get the bacon on".

No one had got the matches. It was the only thing they had forgotten. Still, sweets and chocolate for breakfast aren't the worst thing in the world.

"Let's go and have a look – see if it's still up." Dave was already getting his bike from behind the tent.

It was that time of the day when you feel you have the whole world to yourself and the sun is shining and nothing can go wrong. They cycled to the windmill and, sure enough, the line was still there, complete with washing. They looked at each other, smiled and saluted, then rode back to the main road. Behind them the washing fluttered in the early morning breeze. And just between the boxes and the bales something else fluttered. A white handkerchief. With the initials W.E.T.

They didn't go back to the tent. They turned right. Part two of the plan. They had the road to themselves. Completely. Nothing at all.

"On a clear day you can see Worksop." Nev had stopped at the top of Leverton Hill.

"Yeah. Exciting, eh?" replied Lee.

"Are we going to do it?" asked Donno.

"You bet!" grinned Dave.

Leverton Hill. Steep and unforgiving. Steep and dangerous. All their parents had told them never to ride their bikes down there. Steep – yes. Dangerous – yes. Exciting – absolutely.

"All for one … and one for aaaaaaaaaaaaall!"